Queen of
Schnapps

Also by Tina D.C. Hayes

ROCK CANDY ROMANTIC SUSPENSE
Nefarious

PETAL PUSHERS MYSTERY SERIES
Poison, Perennials, and a Poltergeist
Secrets, Snapdragons, and a Spirit
Grudges, Goldenrods, and Ghosts

Novellas
No More Tears
Valentino, Be Mine

Short Stories
"Midnight Reveille"

Queen of Schnapps

Tina D. C. Hayes

Hazy Moon Ink

ISBN-13: 978-0692717851
ISBN-10: 0692717854

Hazy Moon Ink

Prologue

Larry Fulkerson tipped up his Budweiser can before he tossed more limbs into the wood chipper he'd rented for the week. He knew it would take a while to get rid of the big oak tree that blew down in the storm, but it wasn't too hard now that he'd sawed off the branches and chopped the trunk into smaller pieces.

He had to set his beer on the ground to pick up a few larger chunks of wood, then squatted down so he could lift with his legs since he didn't want to strain his back. After trudging back to the roaring equipment that sounded like Goliath's can opener crossed with the world's deadliest buzz saw, he tossed in the log and watched metal teeth chew it down to splinters in less than a second.

Huh, he thought, this is actually kind of fun.

The next slice of oak went in the same way. As Larry watched the machine devour it, someone ran up behind him and shoved him in.

Just as his body made contact with the blades, before the machinery totally obliterated him and ended his life, he thought he heard a voice straight from hell.

"Fuck *you*, Fulkerson! This is what happens when you get in my way. Enjoy your stupid wood chipper!"

Chapter One

I became insane, with long intervals
of horrible sanity.
~Edgar Allan Poe

Behind the counter at Gas 'N Go, I sat
bored to death watching the clock slowly
tick down the minutes until my shift would
finally be over. Come on five a.m. The past
two months working here had sucked, and I
hate being a clerk. At least it isn't quite as
bad as my last job selling donuts to a
bunch of damn early birds who expected
me to smile and be polite at the ass crack of
dawn.

The electronic device on the door chimed. Frank Wilkes gave me a quick once over on the way to his station behind the counter, then shook his head. "You know Susan's gonna have a shit fit when she catches you without that name tag again."

"If she was that worried about it, she should've got one with my actual name on it." I looked up at him from my stool as I reached under the counter for a small plastic rectangle. "This," I continued, pointing to the white letters printed on the tacky blue background, "clearly does *not* say Judith Webster, so I have no intention of pinning someone else's crap to my shirt. Susan can stick it up her ass, or she can find somebody named Judy and stick it up hers." I tossed the cheap badge back onto the cluttered shelf hoping to never again set eyes on the stupid thing. "What are you laughing at?"

"Don't get mad, but it cracks me up when you get all pissed off. You make these funny faces and your eyes nearly pop out of your head, but it's kind of cute."

"Now Frank, you know I'm married so stop with the compliments." I held one hand up, palm facing him. Not that I don't like being called cute, but I'd never think about cheating with a co-worker. "I told you—"

"I know, we had that talk last week when I pointed out that you had a price sticker stuck to the seat of your pants." Frank grinned like a moron. "Settle down, I didn't mean anything like that. Sometimes I can't tell when you're joking." He winked, but then rubbed his eye. Good thing he caught himself or I'd have been all over him for making another pass at me. "Hey, at least I know better than to call you the wrong name."

"Thanks, Frank, I appreciate that."

I like my name. Judith. It sounds sophisticated and worldly. My biggest pet peeve is having stupid people adulterate it to some dippy nickname like Judy, or worse yet, Jude, both of which I refuse to answer to. If Ed McMahon's ghost ever rang my doorbell with a ginormous check made out to Judy Webster, I'd slam the door in his face. I've explained it to my boss a million and one times, but still, Susan keeps on calling me Judy—possibly to get a rise out of me since I'm apparently so damn adorable when I'm pissed off. No way in hell I'm wearing that fucking plastic tag.

I punched my time card, yelled "See ya tomorrow, Frank," and helped myself to a Heath bar on the way out of the convenience store. The two tones of the chime sounded like a robotic donkey as the door closed behind me.

I wished it was later in the day when I drove past Corkers, my favorite liquor store, on the way home. Some ridiculous law prohibited the sale of alcohol before eight o'clock in the morning, but I had a pretty strong hankering for a nice mind-numbing drink. Maybe I could find something in the back of the kitchen cabinet to hold me over.

The beautiful autumn morning made

me decide to drive through Atkinson Park, located just a few miles from the Gas 'N Go in the heart of Henderson, Kentucky. Trees along the curving pavement arched into a canopy overhead as I drove my blue Buick through a red, gold, and brown confetti of leaves. I parked near the picnic area to eat the candy bar before I started the thirty-minute drive home, the windows down to let in the cool breeze as sunrise blended into the bluing sky.

The Ohio River shimmered below the twin bridges as I drove into the sprawling city of Evansville, Indiana and my upper-middle-class neighborhood on the far side of town. The apple-red front door I painted last Labor Day complemented the tan siding and dark green shutters.

Greg was sound asleep in bed when I got home. His alarm usually went off at six thirty so he had a few more minutes left to snooze.

Our schedules kept us apart most of the time. Greg worked day shift at a factory in town so with me working nights, it was rare for us both to have a whole day to spend together. We did good to have a couple of hours in the evening home at the same time, which we usually spent eating supper in front of the television. We'd been married for sixteen years, so there really wasn't anything all that exciting left to talk about.

I went straight to the kitchen to make breakfast. My mother-in-law would throw up if she saw the stack of unwashed pans and crusty plates in the sink or the filthy drinking glasses on the countertop. The refrigerator, on the other hand, was immaculate. I'd spent the previous Saturday throwing out fuzzy green fruit and veggies and oozing containers of leftover take-out, then scrubbed the shelves with bleach and wiped down all the condiments before I put them back on the shelves. In alphabetical order, of course.

I dropped a couple cherry pop tarts in the toaster for Greg before taking my bacon and eggs to the living room. My black and white cat, drawn by the smell of food, jumped up on the sofa to purr for a bite of my breakfast. I clicked the remote a few times, then cooed down at my kitty. "Good morning, Miss Poopsie. Would you like some of Mama's bacon?" She gobbled up the crispy pieces I put on the sofa cushion along with some scrambled egg bits. "Did you miss me while I was gone, slaving away at that stupid job?" She licked the plate clean after I finished eating.

The cat nuzzled my cheek as I picked her up and headed toward the bedroom. The alarm had gone off a few minutes before so I wasn't surprised to meet Greg on his way to the kitchen.

"Morning, Judith," he said, giving me a quick peck on the cheek as we brushed past each other in the narrow hall. "You make coffee yet?"

"Nope, caffeine would just keep me awake. See ya tonight. Don't work too hard." I went to bed, tucking myself in at about same time Greg pushed the lever to start his pop tarts toasting. Poopsie rested on a satin pillow beside me. Aliens are afraid of cats, so I had no reason to worry about an unwanted anal probe with her purring away.

Chapter Two

Insanity is often the logic of an accurate
mind overtasked.
~Oliver Wendell Holmes, Sr.

By three o'clock that afternoon, I was wide awake, lounging in the living room recliner. Popping dry Fruit Loops into my mouth, I hummed along to the theme song when my favorite soap opera came on. Unless something earth-shattering happened, my happy ass watched *Heartbeats and Teardrops* every weekday afternoon, just as I—their biggest and most loyal fan ever—had for the past eleven years, starting with the premiere episode.

When they cut to the first commercial, I ran to the kitchen to pour myself a drink. Sometimes I added fruit juice or lemon-lime soda or whatever else sounded good at the moment. The time I mixed pickle juice with the Margarita-flavored schnapps had really sucked, but other than that, I was usually pretty pleased with my schnappstails. Today there were only a couple fingers of Hot Damn in the back of the cabinet, my least favorite flavor since it burned my mouth. Better than nothing. I let the red cinnamon liquid flow over the ice cubes before I filled the glass the rest of the way with sweet tea from the pitcher in the fridge. The taste was less than scrumptious, so I added a splash of lemon juice, gave it a stir with an old swizzle stick from Red Lobster, and then hurried back to the television.

The commercial ended as I settled my butt into the recliner and raised the foot-rest. For the next forty-five minutes, I sat mesmerized as the never-ending saga unfolded on the screen. I was happy for the married lady who discovered she was pregnant and couldn't wait to see whether the father turned out to be the woman's husband or the pizza guy. A smarmy dark-haired man started an affair with a nurse from the intensive care unit of the same hospital where his comatose wife had been a patient for the long and lonely past three days. A few of my favorite villains were planning to murder someone but didn't mention who.

The camera focused on the back of a tall blond man with an Irish accent telling a nurse he wanted to see his sister, who turned out to be the scorned woman in the coma. After the nurse pointed down the hall and told him she was in room 407, he turned around for a close-up.

The last green Fruit Loop fell out of my mouth as my jaw dropped. The foot rest snapped closed and I scooted to the edge of the seat for a closer look at the gorgeous soap opera Adonis. This handsome new character's name is Evan Gallagher, long-lost foreign-born illegitimate half-brother to Sylvia Carmichael. With his square jaw, twinkling green eyes, and devilish smile, I knew without a doubt he was the most beautiful man ever to walk the planet.

"Stay tuned for scenes from tomorrow's episode of *Heartbeats and Teardrops*, right after these messages," said the faceless announcer with the deep, soothing voice. Three giggling teenage girls took over the screen, gleefully discussing the baby powder scent of their maxi pads.

"Oh my God!" I'd always been in the habit of talking to myself when no one was around. If I caught myself doing it when Greg was home, I'd just pretend to be talking to the cat, or sometimes I'd play it off like I was singing a song.

My heart beat a wild cadence in my ears. Overcome by a surge of energy, I paced back and forth as I drained the last drop of my Hot Damn iced tea. When tomorrow's preview started, I rushed back to my seat hoping to see a lengthy clip of this Evan Gallagher. Disappointed when they only flashed his face for a split second, I, though still in a euphoric mood, clicked the remote and then threw it across the room. Fortunately, it landed on the sofa and didn't break. Greg always pitched a fit when the remote controls got broke.

I rummaged through cabinets for something to drink, but since I'd just drained the last of my schnapps collection, a few beers in the bottom of the refrigerator were all that was left. I hate the taste of beer but guessed I'd have to make do. I popped open the ice cold can and headed for the computer.

The studly new character had debuted on my soap without any prior advertising to hype his arrival, so I had no clue what his real name was. Unlike movies and every other show on TV, soaps ran credits at the beginning of the program instead of the end. "What fool came up with that stupid idea," I muttered as I typed 'Evan Gallagher' in the Google box near the top of the monitor, then clicked the cursor on the little red button to start the search.

I skimmed the resulting links. The first was a site advertising Gallagher tires, and the next two were for Evan Gall hemorrhoid cream. I rolled my eyes, then tried googling 'Heartbeats and Teardrops Evan Gallagher'.

"Yes!" A link for an article on the Soap Bubbles website topped the list. I clicked it, then chewed my lip impatiently while the page loaded. A big swig of beer made me wish I'd told Greg to stop at the liquor store yesterday.

I scrolled down the page until I came to the 'Making News' section, where I visually fondled the color picture of my new hero. It took some effort to tear my eyes away from his dreamy image long enough to read the paragraph beside the photo.

Today, viewers of Heartbeats and Teardrops got their first peek at a handsome new leading man. Lucas Murphy, a thirty-two-year-old heartthrob in his native Ireland, debuted this afternoon as Evan Gallagher. Only time will tell what mischief he'll get himself into in Eldridge.

The pissy little article didn't tell me much, so I clicked to the bios page. I scanned through the endless list of soap stars, disappointed to reach the bottom of the web page where bold red letters promised the biography of Lucas Murphy would be posted sometime in the near future.

I hit the back button and scrolled back down to the picture of Evan. He wore a denim shirt that brought out the deepest hues of green in his eyes, and the rolled-up sleeves on his crossed arms showed muscles rippling beneath the fabric. Sunshine illuminated his golden hair. His mischievous grin was the most captivating of all.

After a few minutes in Photoshop, the printer gave birth to a glossy wallet-size picture of my new obsession. I rummaged through a box of scrapbooking tools until I found the scissors. Humming the theme song to the daytime drama, I trimmed around the portrait, the small pinking shears creating a border of perfect little hearts along the edges. I finished off the last of the nasty beer, pitched the crushed can into the wastebasket by the desk, and headed back to the living room.

I proudly inserted my art project into my wallet, admiring how it looked sandwiched between my driver's license and a snapshot of Miss Poopsie on Santa's lap. Now I'd have something nice to look at while passing the time at my stupid boring job tonight.

There were a couple of hours left until I had to leave for work, so I decided to cook a nice meal. Singing along to the kitchen radio, I shook salt and pepper over two steaks before I stuck them in the oven and then added a few foil-wrapped potatoes after they'd been pre-nuked in the microwave. Not wanting to see all those messy dishes in the sink while I ate, I loaded the dishwasher. I didn't want to catch a venereal disease from the taco scraps, so I put on my yellow rubber gloves before I held my breath and scraped the plates over the trashcan.

Delicious smells filled the house as I emptied a salad bag into a wooden bowl, set the table, and relaxed.

Gregory Webster certainly was surprised when he got home that night. His wife, dressed in a St Patrick's Day apron, greeted him at the door with a big hug, during which he surveyed the room. No broken glass, no upholstery stuffing scattered around, the cat was still alive, and he saw the remote still intact on the coffee table. Judith had actually cooked and set the table! His Judith, the woman who considered a tuna sandwich with cheese puffs, a candy bar, and one of her weird cocktails to be a hearty meal.

Most of Judith's quirky habits amused him. They were just part of the strong personality that made her the person she was.

Laid back and easy going himself, he liked the way she spoke her mind when the occasion arose and didn't give a damn what other people thought.

She hadn't gone through any of her bad spells for a while. Greg's life had been nearly perfect these past few months while she busied herself with her various hobbies. She was an avid soap opera fan, lived to play the roulette wheel, spent hours shopping on eBay, and maybe she did drink a little too much schnapps, but all that was fine with him. She was a loyal and faithful wife. Not much of a housekeeper, but he'd learned to live with that. He loved Judith just the way she was.

"You know," Judith purred as they finished their dinner, "I have a few minutes before I have to leave." She ran her fingers seductively over the shamrocks on her apron. "In case you're feeling romantic..."

Some of Gas 'N Go's regular customers noticed I was a bit friendlier than usual. Instead of my typical blunt delivery of the purchase total, I preceded it with "that'll be." A few even heard me add little pleasantries such as "thank you" and "come again." Although I still didn't actually smile at the patrons, I made eye contact without making annoyed faces at most of them.

Graveyard shift gave me plenty of down time. The time slot came with extra duties attached to it, like straightening crap on the shelves, cleaning the slushie machine, and dusting off the lottery ticket display. I was supposed to mop the floor and clean the bathroom but only did it when I knew the boss would be coming in at the end of my shift, which hardly ever happened. Bad enough I had to work at this dump, I damn well wasn't going to act like a maid. Screw that. If asked why the cleaning wasn't done—when one of the whiny bitches from day shift complained to Susan about it—I'd arrange my face in an innocent mask of confusion and say I'd indeed mopped and washed up, left everything sparkly clean, and that somebody must have come in after I got off work and left those dirty tampons on the bathroom floor or poured the grape slushie over the motor oil display. Then whose fault was it? I always just shook my head and said it wasn't me.

Things slowed to a dribble after 1 a.m. I helped myself to a fountain drink and a bag of sour cream and onion chips, perks I felt entitled to for keeping this stupid job, and grabbed the newest edition of *Soap Opera Digest* before sitting down on my perch near the cash register. I hadn't been a fan of the magazine since three years ago when they ran that story about Veronica Slater—winner of an Emmy for her role as Jillian Merriweather—leaving *Heartbeats and Teardrops*. Even though the actress had gone through a nervous breakdown stemming from alcoholism, I felt like it was the magazine's fault she'd left the show. They'd been first to cover the story about her leaving for 'personal reasons', which opened the door for every TV journalist in the country. Poor Ms. Slater hadn't been able to go to the ladies' room without flashbulbs exploding all around her when she left the stall, reporters scribbling down how many times she'd wiped her ass. And all those ridiculous interviews with her psychiatrists, as if anyone could trust those fuckers. The sanest person in the world could get a psychological evaluation and leave with at least two mental illnesses on their permanent medical records, not to mention that an occasional cocktail or being on prescription medication let shrinks brand people as alcoholic dope addicts. I'd had enough experience with those crackpots to ever believe a word they had to say.

I thumbed through the pages, pausing to read any snippet involving *Heartbeats and Teardrops* in hopes of finding mention of Evan Gallagher. For some reason, I hadn't been able to get his face out of my mind since it flashed across the television screen a couple days before. Midway through the publication I hit pay dirt. My index finger poked the small photo as if to keep it from disappearing. Actually, the headshot was so tiny my fingertip covered it completely, the realization of which made me quickly move it so I wouldn't smudge his image. Apparently the PR people didn't want to give away very much about this new actor, probably to build intrigue and sell more issues after more viewers had a chance to notice him. There was only a short caption under his photo that said Irishman Lucas Murphy would play Evan Gallagher on *Heartbeats and Teardrops*.

"Well, I already knew that." I flipped through the pages, once again on a quest for more info about my new crush.

"Can you give me the total then, lady, so I can pay for this stuff?" For all the good it'd done, a man had stood there for a full three minutes and mumbled something about gas from pump four, not that I gave a shit. "Not that I want to drag you away from your fashion magazine, but it's late and I'd rather go home instead of standing here all night." He shoved the generic six-pack and a package of tic-tacs across the counter.

I'd been so enthralled with Evan's picture that I hadn't paid attention to this guy before a second ago. I scowled at him and set the tabloid on the stool, still warm from my butt, before I rang up his items. Ready to send this asshole on his merry way, I spoke in a much more hostile tone than I used earlier that evening. "Five ninety-three."

"For the third goddamn time, I got gas from pump four! Are you gonna ring it up or is it going to be an early fuckin' Christmas present?" His stinky breath smacked me in the face as his eyes scanned my smock. Oh great, he was just the type of stupid jerk who'd get off on making up stuff about me to report to the manager. More reason not to wear a name tag.

I sneered at him as I punched numbers on the register, fighting the strong urge to throw the rest of my drink in his ugly face. "Okay, it's twenty-five ninety-three," I said, tilting my head slightly from left to right a couple of times, my voice sing-songing with attitude. "My name is Jennifer."

He banged thirty dollars on the counter, a gesture I mimicked when I slammed his change down a few seconds later. We stared each other down like WWF wrestlers waiting for the signal to go at it. He finally picked up his beer and moved toward the door.

"Don't forget your tic-tacs." I tossed them at his head. "Wise buy, since your breath smells like you ate a shit sandwich for dinner."

Unfortunately, he caught the box of mints before they hit him, then called me a bitch as he left.

I slid open the window and flipped him the bird. "Thank *you* and have a nice day!"

The asshole frowned at me as he drove off in his turd-brown Ford pickup.

Rather than put me in a bad mood, this

encounter made me feel empowered, as if the world was better for my having put that son of a bitch with the shit breath in his place. I returned to the stool to stare at Evan Gallagher's picture and daydreamed my way through the rest of the shift.

Chapter Three

Though this be madness,
yet there is method in't.
~William Shakespeare

"I Feel Lucky" boomed through the speakers as I strolled through the corridor that led me aboard the Tropicana, Evansville's own three-story riverboat casino. With a spring in my step and this week's cashed paycheck in my purse, I was ready to let the good times roll. All I needed now was a nice stiff drink and a seat at one of the gaming tables.

The crowd wasn't too thick tonight, due

to the concert going on over at Ford Center. Some country band I'd never heard of was playing to an audience full of locals, which worked out fine for me since I only had to wait ten minutes for a seat to open at the roulette table. Luckily, this one had a five-dollar minimum so I knew I'd be playing for a while. It wasn't much fun the time I'd waited an hour to get in at the table on the other floor only to learn it had a fifty-dollar minimum, which meant that amount and not one chip less had to be bet by each player each time the wheel spun. Playing for higher stakes was a trip, but I'd left the table three thousand dollars poorer. Greg screamed himself purple before he cut up my credit card when he got that bill. Well, screw him. The whole reason I kept my crappy job was to earn spending money for life's necessities: gambling, eBay, and my schnapps collection.

"Two hundred in small chips, please," I said, beaming as I plopped my money down on the table. The dealer—who really was more of a ball spinner and bet taker, but had that title nonetheless—slid me a mountain of chips. To avoid confusion over which chips were whose, each player received a different color. Mine were a pretty apple green tonight. I meticulously arranged them in front of me, in eight tidy stacks of twenty-five, three rows deep, with the short row of two stacks in back.

Statistically, my odds of winning went up each time I bet the same numbers, as opposed to picking random ones with each spin. With that in mind, I always bet the exact same numbers each round, every time I sat down to play. I could only remember losing badly when I'd impulsively decided to play different numbers at the end of a run. I pulled a small green memo pad from my purse and flipped through a few wrinkled pages until I came to my lucky numbers.

Not wanting to put a chip on the wrong square, I quickly read through my list and the little poem written below it. Seven and eleven topped the page because they were mentioned in some cool songs about gambling and were important in craps, a game I found too confusing to play. Next came nineteen, the number of cats I'd had over my lifetime, followed by twenty-one, the magical age of legal drinking. Last but not least was thirty-four, the number of delicious flavors available in my favorite drink of all time, schnapps. I bet five dollars on each of these five numbers each spin, knowing I'd win a hundred and seventy-five bucks each time the little ball landed in one of the corresponding spaces on the roulette wheel. I bet the color red when I had a strong gut feeling, or when it hadn't come up for more than five spins in a row. An outside bet, red cost an additional Lincoln when I felt the need to put my chips on the red square located on the side of the table. I never bet on black as a color because it was the symbol of death, evil, and rotting vegetables, shit nobody in their right mind would put money on.

Before tucking my memo pad back into my purse, I tore out a clean sheet and folded it a few times until it was roughly the size of a teabag. I placed this and a two-inch long nubbin of a pencil on the table in front of me, concealing it with my left hand so other people couldn't figure out what I was doing and horn in on my good luck by copying my strategy. Tally marks on the paper helped keep count of how many spins I'd bet on. I always stopped at the sacred number thirty-three, the age of Jesus when he died. Practically the only time I prayed was during these gambling sessions, so it didn't hurt to suck up to the man upstairs by using a holy number in my system.

Careful not to actually speak the words to the little poem out loud as I recited it in my head, I picked up one stack of chips from the front row on the left end. Standing up to better reach around the table, I placed five chips on each number as I came to them in my poem: seven and eleven, take me to heaven; nineteen, make me a queen;

twenty-one, let's have us some fun; thirty-four, a winner for sure. I sat back down, feeling pretty confident as I marked my first tally and waited for the ball to land.

When the cocktail waitress came around, I ordered Jack and Coke. Obviously, I'd prefer something with schnapps and maybe a little fruit juice mixed in, but the boat served a limited selection of booze, mainly beer and hard liquor, without any frilly foo-foo concoctions. Nevertheless, my night brightened as soon as I took the first sip. I set the plastic cup in its place in front of me, a couple inches in front of and to the right of my chips, three inches from the tally sheet.

The ball slowed down and hopped around the wheel like a silver jumping bean. I crossed my fingers and waited to see where it would land.

"Twenty-four," the dealer announced as she set the glass marker on the black square adorned with that number. An older lady wearing an Elvis shirt woo-hooed.

Some guy across from me took off his John Deere cap and proceeded to stomp on it several times. I took a swig of my Jack and Coke wondering why the man wore that hat in the first place, if he hated it so much.

The dealer raked the losing bets aside, doled out the winning chips to the Elvis fan and an Asian man seated at the corner, then removed the glass marker. "Place your bets." Players scrambled to decorate the table top with plastic polka dots as the dealer launched the ball on its new orbit around the roulette wheel. The rapid tick-tick-tick gradually slowed until the dealer waved her hands over the table and said, "No more bets." Seconds later, she broadcast where the little ball landed. Cheers and groans sounded as the red number eighteen lit up on the board behind the wheel end of the table.

Thirty-four, a winner for sure. Making the third tally mark, I hoped this spin went in my favor, since I'd just plucked down my seventy-fifth chip. I lived comfortably in a nice house with a two car garage so it wasn't like I was desperate for money. I just liked to win, and the adrenaline rush that came with it. Absentmindedly playing with my necklace, I glanced around the room for the ditsy cocktail girl who should've brought my next drink by now.

"Twenty-one," called the dealer.

I looked from the glass marker to the lighted board to make sure I'd heard correctly. "Oh yeah!"

The Elvis lady high-fived me as the dealer heaped a hundred and seventy-five chips around my apple-green disk. What a high! I restacked the chips into neat little piles of twenty-five. Things got even better when my much anticipated second cup of Jack and Coke arrived.

Loosening up a little, I bobbed my head in time to the golden oldies that filled the room. Three Dog Night sang about Jeremiah the bullfrog a few spins later when I won ten dollars for betting red, even though a nine came up instead of one of my numbers. Not as big a deal as the other win, but my adrenaline pumped all the same.

About the time I made my twelfth tally mark, I noticed I was down to a hundred and fifteen chips, quite a drop from the three hundred and twenty-five I'd counted after the first win. Not ready to go back to my boring house just yet, I said a silent prayer, sliding the locket back and forth on its gold chain as I waited to see where the ball went next.

"Oh yeah!" I cheered when the dealer called my number. "Nineteen, made me a queen!" I raised my new lucky charm, the locket clutched in my hand, and kissed it.

The bouncing Elvis fan also had chips on nineteen. She stopped jumping up and down long enough to give me a congratulatory hug before we raked in our piles of loot.

When I had to pee so badly I was afraid I'd wet myself, I asked Emma, the Elvis lady, to save my seat. I had to circle the room twice before I found the right table on my way back, gloriously refreshed after relieving my bladder of about a gallon of piss, so I decided to slack off on drinks for a few spins. Since I had to drive home, I abstained for a whole hour before my next drink, a cold Miller Genuine Draft, just like my new buddy Emma drank.

"Hey, Emma, they're playing your song," I said when Mr. Presley's "Jailhouse Rock" poured through the speakers. We clinked our beer cans together. "Cheers."

My hoard of plastic pucks had dwindled down to four piddling stacks, just enough for four more losing rounds. I crossed through my fifth set of tally marks, hoping to improve my chances of staying in the game until the sacred thirty-third spin, still eight whirls away. I slid my locket back and forth a few times, hoping it would work its lucky magic spell once again.

An impulse urged me to open my talisman as the ball whizzed around the wheel. The locket housed the picture torn from *Soap Opera Digest*, carefully cut to fit the tiny oval frame. I soon became lost in daydreams of Evan Gallagher as I stared at his image.

"Is that your husband?" Emma peered over my shoulder at the small photo. "What gorgeous green eyes he has!"

"Yep, he's my sweetie," I gushed, still lost in my daydream. When I realized what she'd just said, my ears started to burn as a blush warmed my face.

"You're a lucky woman to have him to go home to." Emma patted my shoulder. "Hey, she's fixing to put that glass thingy down. Come on, twenty-eight. Mama needs a new pair of blue suede shoes!"

"Lucky number seven . . . for the first time tonight, I think," the dealer said.

"Yeah baby!" My cheers drew attention from the Asian gentleman who'd just lost a grand when double zero failed to be called. He sneered in my direction, so I glared back until he quit looking at me and the tally sheet hidden under my hand. The dealer piled a hundred and seventy-five apple green smackeroos in front of me. No way could I lose it all before I had to call it a night. Only seven more spins left.

Two epiphanies popped into my now barely buzzing brain as I shuffled my chips around. First and most obvious, the locket enshrining Evan's picture had proved itself to be a lucky charm. I'd touched it each time the little ball bounced onto one of my winning numbers. I silently vowed never again to take it off my neck.

The second realization was definitely the sweetest, the possibilities boggling my mind as I sat there in the haze of the busy casino, stuck in a strange state somewhere between a daydream and cognitive thought. Emma assumed Evan was my husband, that I, Judith Ann Webster, was actually capable of marrying a man of his caliber. I'd been smitten by the hunky Irishman ever since I first laid eyes on him, his manly features filling the television screen like a ray of fresh Egyptian sunshine. Somewhere deep down in my soul I'd known it all along, but had been too afraid to let the idea form in my mind in case things didn't work out. Tonight, though, it was as plain to see as the purple fanny pack wrapped around Emma's waist. I was destined to meet, marry, and spend the rest of my life with Evan Gallagher.

"You'd better hurry up with those chips, 'cause I think she's fixin' to wave her hand over the table," Emma warned, drawing my attention back to the roulette wheel. Reciting the poem in my head, I managed to get my bet on the table in the nick of time, for all the good it did. I didn't have any money riding on the black two that flashed on the board behind the dealer.

As I finished off my last drink, I won another mound of money when the glass marker was again placed on the red square labeled twenty-one. That time, me and Emma celebrated by dancing the cabbage patch followed with a butt bump, all to the tune of Bobby Brown's "My Prerogative".

The dealer raised an eyebrow at us,

and the Asian man looked like he was going to puke. They were so jealous.

Chapter Four

Everything great in the world is done by neurotics; they alone founded our religions and created our masterpieces.
~Marcel Proust

Sunday was my day off. After soaking in a steamy bubble bath that morning, I enjoyed the luxury of wearing flannel pajamas and fluffy pink slippers around the house all day.

I'd left the boat Friday night with a little over four hundred bucks, double what I arrived with, even after all the drinks I bought. I barely remembered the drive home, but I'd made it safe and sound so that's all that really mattered.

I invested some of my winnings during Saturday's trip to Corkers. Everyone who worked there knew me by name and made sure to tell me when they got in new flavors of my favorite brands. I'd spent a hundred dollars on a scrumptious assortment of schnapps and brought home a variety of bottles in three sizes.

Not one to let money burn a hole in my pocket, I also made a trip to the Walmart on my side of town. I bought enough candles to light the house up for the next twenty years or so, should electricity ever cease to exist in the free world; that could happen any day now, whenever the communists enacted their plan to storm Area 51. Some knock-off brand of laptop was on sale for half-price, an offer Judith Webster sure couldn't refuse. Then I piled five velvety purple and gold journals, two agenda books for the upcoming year, and an armload of notepads into the shopping cart along with a few packs of gel pens in a rainbow of colors.

After mixing up apple schnapps, Sierra Mist, and a maraschino cherry, I sauntered to the spare bedroom where we keep the computer. I logged onto my eBay account, typed in 'Queen_of_Schnapps' as my user name and 'whoopee' for the password, and then waited for the page to load.

I spent the next few hours looking at bargains from across the globe, trying to make up my mind which items to bid on. I absolutely love eBay, my favorite place to shop for nearly everything from collectibles to life's necessities. Once, I'd been the winning bidder on a perfectly good box of unopened tampons for only a quarter. I got such a kick from outbidding other people on things, the competitive aspect only added to the fun. On days I couldn't stand to wait for a bid to end, I'd take the 'Buy it Now' option. It would be cool to actually sell some stuff on there, but I hadn't yet gotten around to it. I could make a bundle auctioning off the old stuff Greg had cluttering up the place.

Before surfing away from eBay, I managed to make some great deals. Just in time for the upcoming holiday season, I had a four-dollar bid in on a Snoopy snow globe with a tiny Charlie Brown beside his Red Baron disguised beagle inside the snowy plastic bubble. I'd have to wait two more days to see who'd win the privilege of purchasing the blown glass swizzle sticks; I really needed to win that auction, since I was sick of stirring my drinks with crappy plastic ones from local restaurants that featured Happy Hour specials. I'm a real sucker for a bargain.

I only made one instant purchase that afternoon, something I couldn't pass up after reading the description underneath the picture of the item offered by BargainKitty57 of Tulsa, Oklahoma. Made of velvet-covered foam and shaped like a giant orange goldfish, the deluxe domed cat bed was lined with luxurious silky fabric and came with a purple cushion embossed with images of more teensy little fish. Just imagine how cute Miss Poopsie would be, sitting all cozy inside her new naptime hideaway, looking almost as if the fish with the charming black sequined eyes had swallowed her up. She didn't seem too enthusiastic when I held her up to the screen to see her present, but I just knew she'd love it. Shipping and all, it only cost a hundred and thirty-seven dollars. Score!

The shopping done for the day, I decided to run another search for my new Romeo. I googled Evan Gallagher and Lucas Murphy, both of the names that belonged to the King of Daytime Drama. Nothing. After a few more tries, I was discouraged to find nothing more than the same small blurb on SoapBubbles.com I'd already seen days before.

I figured that since Ireland was Evan's birthplace, I needed to educate myself on Celtic culture and traditions. He must've seen lots of those leprechauns who inhabited the lush four-leaf clover covered hillsides over there. Chewing on the cherry from my fourth apple schnapps and Sierra Mist schnappstail, I wondered if people kept the mini Irishmen as pets or simply made friends with the strange little creatures.

After a short time in Internet Irish 101, I came to some interesting conclusions. To my great disappointment, leprechauns were not in fact real. That sure sucked! At least the Irish pubs sounded like something that would be right up my alley, and I made a note in the Hello Kitty journal I kept in the desk drawer to buy some Guinness beer the following week. The sound bites of traditional music sounded alright, in a folksy sort of way, so if Evan put in a CD of the stuff, I guessed I could handle listening to it. The River Dancing shit, however, I could totally do without.

One thing that captivated me was the shillelagh, the stick-like possession of traditional Irishmen and the fictitious leprechauns (I was still pretty bummed out over that disappointing discovery). At first glance they appeared to be walking sticks, but were actually nifty handcrafted weapons. Irish people carried them around to whop each other over the head with whenever they got good and pissed off. After reading up on those, I surfed back over to eBay. The winning forty-four dollar bid for an authentic blackthorn shillelagh I'd found a couple minutes before the auction ended went to . . . me, Judith Ann Webster, the Queen of Schnapps.

I made a note in my memo pad to set the alarm next week so I'd be awake when the mailman made his rounds. I loved getting packages in the mail and simply couldn't wait to open the shillelagh. And Miss Poopsie's new goldfish bed!

Chapter Five

*I quite agree with Dr Nordau's assertion
that all men of genius are insane, but Dr
Nordau forgets that all sane people are idiots.*
~Oscar Wilde

"Damn it!"

"Sorry Mrs. Webster. You're not the first person to get a little miffed when things travel down the postal highway slower than expected. Maybe it'll come tomo—"

I slammed my lovely red front door shut, narrowly missing the mailman's arm in the process. Outside on the porch, Harry Qualls jumped back in time to escape injury, unfortunately. The jackass strolled on down the sidewalk whistling a happy tune as he readied the envelopes for the Andersons three doors down. Maybe he wouldn't screw them over.

"The damn thing is still not here yet!" I banged the bills he'd given me onto the coffee table, then soothed myself with a draw from my glass of tropical-flavored schnapps and pineapple juice. I swirled the ice cubes around with one of my new swizzle sticks, the delicate blown glass wands I'd bought from eBay. They were in the only package that spiteful mailman had brought all week, just to torment me. Six whole days since I'd purchased the shillelagh and Poopsie's goldfish bed, so why the hell hadn't he delivered them yet? I even met Harry at the door each day, for all the good it did. Now I'd have to wait until Monday afternoon before it could possibly get here.

While I looked forward to sending my mom a postcard of Poopsie playing in the belly of her new cat bed, I really wanted to get my hands on that Celtic club eBay's description had promised to be carved from some of the finest blackthorn wood Ireland had to offer. I had no idea what a blackthorn tree looked like or what was so special about it, but if my new shillelagh was made out of it, it must be some damn fine wood.

I'd spent quite a bit of time during the past week studying up on the Irish martial arts weapon. Some idiots advertised shillelaghs as canes or walking sticks, but that was just wrong. I ordered a training manual from Amazon.com that promised to be chock full of photographs and detailed information to help me learn how to wield the twenty-three inch club also known as a bata. A person could use this nifty stick to pommel the daylights out of their enemies, and there were ways to make it even more potent. A loaded stick, like the description of mine from the eBay page, meant the knob end had been hollowed out and filled with molten lead. It would really pack a wallop. I couldn't wait to get my hands on that shillelagh! There were times I'd even daydreamed more about it than Evan Gallagher.

One valuable piece of information from Wikipedia would save me from embarrassing myself around all the Irish folks I planned to meet in the near future. My pronunciation had been completely off, but who could have guessed it from the weird way the word was spelled? The object I'd been calling a "shu-lel-lug" actually had a much more poetic pronunciation of "shu-lay-la", which sounded much better. Saying it over and over again, I decided that if I ever had a baby girl, I'd definitely call her Shillelagh Rose. I hoped Evan would like that name.

Another nugget I'd learned was that the Irish-brewed Guinness beer was a keg apart from the good ole American stuff Greg chugged down while cheering on those stupid football players on Monday nights. It was pricier, which I'd found out Tuesday when I picked up a case of the rustic bottles at Corkers. The Irish stuff had a much prettier brownish amber color to it and a more robust smell, both of which met my approval. As far as taste was concerned, I was still undecided. The first bottle was too bitter and thick, with a sort of pissy aftertaste. At least I could drink a classic MGD without making a face, but not this stuff. The second bottle went down a little smoother, and I sort of remembered liking the third one. I had to switch back to my spearmint schnapps after that last one, though, to get that odd taste out of my mouth after I had the sensation of swallowing a stray piece of hops, which Greg had assured me was quite impossible. I saved the rest for this weekend to retest it, so I'd probably uncap one before the sun sat on this lovely Saturday afternoon.

I clicked through channels until I ran across a program on SoapNet summarizing the high points from the last five episodes of *Heartbeats and Teardrops*. The host would show clips, add more details about events surrounding it, and sometimes drop clues as to what the future might hold for some of the more popular inhabitants of Eldridge, USA. I'd obviously seen all the episodes the show was about to cover, but, not wanting to miss an opportunity to see Evan Gallagher's devilish grin, glued my eyes to the set.

Making myself comfortable, I snuggled under the afghan that usually adorned the back of the sofa I lounged on. Down the hall, Miss Poopsie batted a catnip-filled toy mouse back and forth between her paws, the small jingling bell attached to it making enough distraction that I hit the volume button a few times to drown it out.

The program had just come on and host Lynn Baxter was talking about Cynthia DeHaven. After a battery of paternity tests, the obvious two baby daddies had been ruled out. To Cynthia's heart-wrenching disappointment, neither her husband Ed nor Billy Bob, the frisky pizza delivery man who always left a little something extra in the DeHaven household, turned out to be the lucky man. A clip showed Cynthia's mind turning back to a hazy night two months before when she remembered dancing with someone at some sleazy bar, but who? Her mind had been too blurred by the mickey someone secretly put in her martini to recall even the smallest detail of her dance partner . . . except the exquisite scarab-shaped pinky ring on his right hand. The host promised more details about this mystery man would be revealed by next Tuesday's episode.

"Hmmmm. I wonder if it could be James Merriweather." I pondered that over a few sips of schnapps and pineapple juice.

Lynn Baxter recapped recent developments concerning Sylvia Carmichael. A medley of clips showed the lovely woman in a sleep-like state of comatose slumber, her long auburn curls artfully arranged on her pillow in a style that reminded me of a mermaid's hair floating around her head in some beautiful underwater kingdom. Her bastard of a cheating husband looked in on her once while, in the lab a few doors down from his unconscious wife, his nurse friend was busy rebuttoning her blouse. Sylvia's long-lost brother, the handsome Evan Gallagher himself, was shown holding vigil at her bedside, cradling her hand between his, speaking sweetly to her in his sexy accent. As a large portion of the hospital's nursing staff gathered around the doorway to room 407 to listen, a teary-eyed Evan sang a lovely Irish ballad to the sister he believed to be dying. To the amazement of the attending physicians, Sylvia opened her eyes, miraculously called out of the coma by the brother she hadn't seen in the past twenty years.

I wiped away the tear that slipped down my cheek, felt around between the cushions for a tissue, then gave up and blew my nose on the afghan. I was so relieved Sylvia pulled through the ordeal that I'd let emotions get the best of me.

"Who would've guessed Sylvia could bounce back so soon after that horrible car crash?" Lynn's too glossy crimson lips almost looked like they were bleeding in contrast to her over-whitened glow-in-the-dark teeth. "I still wonder what made her swerve off the road in the first place."

Switching gears, talk turned to its newest actor. "Lucas Murphy has been heating up the screen with his laughing Irish eyes, let me tell you." Lynn faked a swoon. "You wouldn't believe how much fan mail has poured into the studio since Lucas made his debut on *Heartbeats and Teardrops* as Evan Gallagher. Looking at his handsome face, it's easy to see why." Sappy violin music played as a montage of close-up stills featuring Evan glided across the television.

The segment took an unexpected turn. A shot of the infamous Merriweathers appeared, minus the music and taking the place of the photo parade that had literally made me drool all over the snotty afghan. I love the Merriweathers! Scene snippets showed them plotting against their next target. Draining the last of my schnappstail I sat up a bit straighter, hoping to find some clue about the identity of this unfortunate person my favorite nasty soap family planned to torment.

Suddenly Poopsie, having abandoned her catnip for a cat nap on the sofa beside me, hissed before jumping from her warm seat to run from the room and take refuge under the bed. The last words from the hostess had upset me so badly and surprised me so much that a fountain of the tropical schnapps and pineapple juice had spewed out of my mouth and all over the poor cat who'd been nestled beside me.

"A little bird flew over the studio to give me a juicy tidbit to share with our loyal audience of soapsters. I have it on good authority that the person the Merriweather family is going to target will be—" Lynn Baxter took a very long, dramatic pause to prolong the agony of her anxious viewers, "—the very handsome Irishman, Evan Gallagher."

Chapter Six

Twinkle, twinkle little bat!
How I wonder where you're at!
Up above the world you fly,
like a tea-tray in the sky.
~Lewis Carroll

When I peeped out the front window on a particularly sunny day the following week, after having stared up and down the sidewalks a few dozen times that afternoon, destiny rewarded my efforts. Harry Qualls was finally strolling up my sidewalk, but the best part, the reason I clapped and giggled like a toddler, was the two packages he took out of his big mailman purse. Harry must have decided to stop being mean and deliver my much anticipated merchandise.

I felt a big stupid grin on my face as I yanked open the front door. "Top of the morning to you, Harry!"

The mailman, still climbing the four steps to the front porch, looked confused at first, but then smiled at me as he stepped up to the doorway. "Well, top of the morning to you too, Mrs. Webster, even if it is the middle of the afternoon a good four months before St. Paddy's day." He handed me the packages with a sale flier and two envelopes piled on top. "I hope these are the eBay deliveries you've been asking me about every single day for the past couple weeks. Have a nice day."

"Thanks Harry! You do the same." I took the parcels, shut the door, and hurried to open them. I requisitioned a wooden-handled steak knife from the butcher's block on the kitchen counter, then, beginning with the larger of the two deliveries, put the tool to work along the taped seams of the cardboard box, using all the delicate care and precision of the world's finest surgeon. I didn't want to nick the contents. The floor around me was soon littered with hundreds of beige packing peanuts, tossed carelessly about as I excavated the contents from the recesses of the box.

"Miss Poopsie, come look at this! Your new bed's here!" My unresponsive cat was snoozing somewhere in the back of the house. The only way sure to make her come running in would've been to crank up the electric can opener, a sound she knew meant tuna in her heart-shaped kitty dish, but I didn't have time for that now.

The feline's lack of compliance didn't faze me in the slightest as I sat on the living room floor, adding to the beige debris accumulating around me as I extracted all the pieces that went to Miss Poopsie's new furniture. I cut off the plastic wrapper that encapsulated the main part of the cat bed and stuck my hand into the goldfish's mouth to snap the domed fish fin roof into shape. Oh, how heavenly the inside lining felt as I ran my hands over the golden orange fabric. The last piece I took from the box was the silky purple cushion, beautifully embossed with teensy baby fish. I laid my own head on this fluffy accessory, just a touch envious of the luxury my cat would soon be napping on. I placed it through the lips of the huge goldfish mouth, settling it in the ample goldfish belly. I took a moment to beam at the fishy magnificence I'd just assembled.

Wanting to share this special moment with someone, I went to retrieve Miss Poopsie. I found her sleeping on top of the dresser in the sunny spot where the sun spilled in through the curtains. I told her all about the surprise waiting for her in the next room as I scooped her up and carried her down the hall.

I suddenly felt silly.

It was technically *not* a surprise, since I'd shown the cat the picture on the computer monitor the day I ordered it. "Anyway, you're gonna love this! Go on," I encouraged, sitting Poopsie down at the entrance of the fish shaped extravagance. "Hop on in and try it out!"

The cat was nowhere near as thrilled about her new digs as I was. She glanced at the thing, then turned to make her way back to the sunny spot in the bedroom where she planned to finish her afternoon nap. I picked her up and poked the squirming cat through the mouth opening, then held her against the fluffy cushion. "It's okay, silly girl," I said, laughing, "you're supposed to be in there. The fishie belongs to you!"

Miss Poopsie was thoroughly unimpressed, still trying to wiggle away and escape, though I'll never understand why.

"Just a sec," I said patiently, an idea forming in my head to help my finicky pet better enjoy her gift.

A few minutes a later, I sat down to relax after I'd duct taped a piece of the cardboard box securely over the mouth of the fish bed, sealing Miss Poopsie inside. She looked so cute sitting in there, peeping through the air holes I'd made in the cardboard, all fluffed up with her ears plastered against her little head.

My attention turned to the smaller box on the coffee table. I'd managed to forget all about it, what with all the fuss over the cat furniture. I picked it up and shook it like a kid trying to decipher whether they had socks or Tinker Toys hidden inside a present. I just knew that packed inside this box was my most prized new possession, handcrafted from Ireland's finest blackthorn wood, my brand new shillelagh! For some reason, the fact that it was no bigger than the box cornflakes came in totally escaped me. I bloody well expected all twenty-three inches of my Celtic club to be tucked in there anyway.

Doing an Irish dance of joy, I jigged over to where I'd left the steak knife, clutching the box to my chest along the way. I perched on the edge of my sofa, placed the sacred vessel on my lap, and set about the same operation-like procedure I'd used to cut open the cat bed that now held Miss Poopsie. With the tape severed around three adjacent edges of the box, I placed the knife on the coffee table and opened the top of the container like a hinged lid. A scant handful of packing peanuts fell around my feet as I lifted out a rectangular object wrapped in brown paper.

A frown puckered my forehead as I peeled away the wrapper and found myself holding *Martial Arts of the Irishman*, the book I'd ordered from Amazon.com. Why had it arrived before the shillelagh? The whole thing simply made no sense. What good was this fucking book going to be when I didn't have the shillelagh it promised to instruct me how to use?

I picked up the recently dissected box from Amazon, turned it upside down and watched hopefully as nothing fell out but a lone Styrofoam peanut. Throwing that box over my shoulder, I retrieved the larger one and removed the rest of the packing material one handful at a time, lest I miss the twenty-three inch long stick of wood I still expected to find there.

"Goddamn it!" I kicked the empty box across the room and yelled more obscenities as I stomped on the Styrofoam bits that littered the carpet. Then something caught my eye. Frozen with one leg lifted like a mountain climber on his way up the side of Mt Everest, I stared at the envelopes on the coffee table. "That no good son of a bitch!" my voice boomed as I sat my foot back down, wishing the lazy mailman was still here so I could've kicked his ass with it instead.

"I've had just about enough of this shit!" Storming into the kitchen to drown my rage in straight peppermint schnapps, I couldn't figure out why the mailman had it in for me. Ice cubes clinked in the high-ball glass as I trudged back to the sofa, searching my brain for any reasonable motive for his cruelty.

I got mad all over again when an image of Harry popped into my mind, parading through the street, pumping my shillelagh up and down like a baton to the beat of his marching feet as if he were leading an invisible band down the center of Main Street.

Harry Qualls was not the nice man I'd once thought him to be. I knew he was lazy a few years ago when he'd been stingy with the Christmas cards . . . until I bribed him with the cocoa. I'd had to meet him at the door each time it snowed or the weather dipped with a steamy cup of goddamn cocoa, an oozy layer of melted marshmallows floating on top. Then, for all my efforts, he finally started bringing my Christmas cards around the second week of December. "You lazy bastard," I hissed.

I took a big sip from my glass.

My pissed off mind conjured up another daydream. Harry Qualls sat in a bar full of postal workers, gleefully entertaining his cohorts with funny stories about how he tormented poor Judith Webster. They knew exactly who I was because he put a framed eight-by-ten of me on the bar right beside his frosty beer mug. He told them all about how he'd dilly-dallied for weeks with my stuff, then delivered the book before the package I was really waiting for. Harry reached under his barstool and pulled out the blackthorn shillelagh. Overcome by hysterical laughter, one of the assholes he worked with spewed beer all over the place as Harry bent over and pointed his behind toward the photograph of me. "Here's the package you've been waiting for, Mrs. Webster!" He acted like he was wiping his boney ass with my precious shillelagh, running it up and down his butt crack! "I'd like my cocoa now please, and don't forget the goddamn marshmallows!"

"Oh, that does it!" I yelled to the living room, empty except for the cat held captive inside the goldfish. "Fuck *you*, Harry Qualls!"

I refilled my peppermint schnapps and

marched over to the fireplace. I was the only person who knew the eighth brick from the right on the third row up from the hearth would slide right out. I wiggled the brick from its spot, reached into the gaping mortar, and removed a spiral bound memo pad with Tweety Bird gracing the cover.

Flipping to a specific page, I was very pleased with myself as I read through the names inscribed there. Using the pencil kept inside the spiral binding, I interjected a hearty "Ha!" and "so there!" as I added Harry Qualls' name ten lines down from Larry Fulkerson's.

Satisfied after that was done, I tucked the Tweety pad safely away back in its cache.

I spent the next few hours reading my new copy of *Martial Arts of the Irishman*. The rest of my Thursday afternoon went much better, now that Harry Qualls was officially on my shit list.

I'd never liked my job at the Gas 'N Go, but today it especially sucked to be me. Stupid bitchy Jennifer from day shift had taken the day off for some ridiculous non-sense—a doctor's appointment or some such crap—and I'd been forced to fill in. So here I was, stuck working Friday afternoon ringing up totals for a parade of assholes buying lottery tickets and fueling up their junky cars and trucks. A pint of schnapps waited in my purse, nerve tonic for when the afternoon rush inevitably poured in.

Hired as a part-time clerk, I normally worked three or four nights a week, nights being the operative word on the job description. The late hours were perfect since I didn't like dealing with people and couldn't stand a crowd standing in line expecting me to wait on their every whim while they bought gas and cigarettes. As a tradeoff for making me come in during daylight hours, I was getting the rest of the weekend off.

Another thing that pissed me off about

working this afternoon was that *Heartbeats and Teardrops* would be on at three o'clock whether I worked or not. Well, I came in prepared with my handy-dandy new laptop bookmarked to the subscription website that simulcast my favorite soap. The next episode was supposed to be especially exciting and I wasn't about to miss a moment of it, the scenes with Evan Gallagher in particular.

I punched keys on the cash register that afternoon, stealing glances at the laptop in its clandestine spot beside me, blocked from the customers' view by the over-sized potato chip display in front of the counter. The volume was low enough that no one noticed it over the usual racket in the store, but, at precisely three o'clock, I hooked up the small earpiece so I wouldn't miss a single word of my beloved soap opera.

Before the first commercial break, I'd waited on four customers while watching Cynthia DeHaven on her psychiatrist's couch during a hypnosis session. In an attempt to figure out the identity of the man who could be her baby's father, an unconscious Cynthia answered all sorts of juicy questions asked by Dr. Melinda Martin. Still no closer to learning who the mystery man was, the viewers in TV land found out that Mrs. DeHaven got a thrill from shoplifting cosmetics from a drug store in Eldridge, went through three lesbian lovers in college during her experimental phase, and didn't like her parents at all.

While a foreign lizard advertised car insurance on the screen, I called to a lady with two small kids hanging off her in the candy isle, "Ready to check out, ma'am?" They were the last people in the store and I hoped to rush them out before the show resumed. My plan succeeded and they were soon on their merry way through the door. "Thanks, and have a nice day!" I said, happy to see them go.

I settled my butt on an old stool beside the cash register as the soap theme called my attention back to the show. Sappy music that somehow managed to sound both romantic and sleazy at the same time played in the background as Blake Carmichael's dark features filled the screen. In the midst of seducing Brandi, the buxom blonde cousin of his last conquest, Becky the ICU nurse, Blake whispered sweet nothings into her ear right when I had to tear my eyes away and place them instead on the rough complexion of a teenage girl.

Her merchandise consisted of pimple cream and mascara. "Walmart has this stuff a whole lot cheaper, and they carry better brands too. Great place to shop." The young shopper left in time for me to catch the tail end of Blake and Brandi's love scene before the next commercial break.

I took a medium-sized slushie cup from the stack beside the drink machine and poured in orange juice until it was three quarters of the way full. Orange schnapps from my purse topped off the cheap cup before I snapped on a lid and stabbed a red straw through the x-shaped slit. I settled back on the stool to enjoy the drink I called OJ's Glove. People would think I was drinking my day's wholesome allowance of vitamin C, but I'd be pulling a fast one, just like a certain brilliant hero of mine fooled the jury when he crammed his hand into a glove that just didn't seem to fit.

On screen, doctors broke the bad news to poor Sylvia Carmichael that she might lose a toe due to complications from the accident that sent her into the coma from which she had so recently recovered. The next scene revealed James, Martha, and Vivian Merriweather planning something awful for Evan Gallagher, which drew my full attention. Apparently, Evan knew too much about the Merriweather's wool business in Dublin. James peered through Evan's window, watching him pour a snifter of brandy—

"Hey, I said I got five dollars' worth from pump three," said a college student wearing a University of Evansville sweatshirt, interrupting the storyline I'd much rather be listening to than him. I took his ten-dollar bill and quickly counted his change.

"Holy shit," I said out loud, though I usually tried to be careful not to talk to myself at work when anyone was around. The college boy was on his way to an out-of-town ball game, and apparently so were the other three carloads that had just pulled into the parking lot. I glanced back at the laptop.

"Oh my God!" James Merriweather aimed a pistol through the window at my unsuspecting Evan!

My mind raced to figure out how to escape the onslaught of football fans as I rang up the next customer. The whorey girls from the second car gossiped by the slushie machine while the people from the third vehicle argued over which brand of beer to take to the stupid game.

With my trusty laptop tucked under my arm and the spiked OJ and a clipboard loaded down with papers in my hands, I ran through the loitering crowd straight to the ladies' room. Locking the door behind me, I threw down the clipboard—which I'd only carried so the customers would think I'd rushed off to take inventory in the back—and sat on the toilet with the laptop balanced on my knees.

As James Merriweather closed his left eye to better aim the pistol, someone knocked on the bathroom door.

"Occupied!" I tilted the laptop at an awkward angle to make the signal come in more clearly.

"We need to pay for our stuff, lady," a female voice said through the grimy door. Probably one of the slutty girls who'd piled out of the second car. Why would she not shut up?

"I'm on my break!"

A close-up of Evan Gallagher appeared on the screen sitting precariously on my lap. Theme music emphasized what I already knew, that something life shattering was just about to happen.

"Um, nobody's at the register," the little

bitch whined through the lock, "so what're we supposed to do?"

"I said I'm on my fucking break! You can shove the shit up your ass, for all I care. Now, leave me the hell alone!"

"But—"

"Thank you and come again." I shoved a finger into the ear that didn't hold the earpiece, hoping to block out any noise that might distract me from the predicament playing itself out on my soap opera.

The screen flipped back and forth between close-ups of James Merriweather flexing his trigger finger and Evan Gallagher sipping brandy, totally unaware of the danger lurking just outside his window.

"No!" I shrieked as a dull pop sounded from Merriweather's gun. Handsome Evan Gallagher lay on the floor, a red splotch marring his silk shirt, his aged brandy spilled across the oriental rug.

I heard the college kids booking ass out of the store, pretty sure they took a bunch of free shit with them. Not that I gave one sweet damn what they did. My eyes were glued to the laptop clutched between my sweaty palms.

Waiting for scenes from Monday's episode, I couldn't believe Evan had been shot. He simply could not die without falling in love with me first!

He simply couldn't. What kind of mixed-up world was this?

When previews for next week didn't reveal a thing about Evan's health, I became more distraught. A fog of hopelessness gnawed at my soul.

Chapter Seven

There's a fine line between genius and insanity. I have erased this line.
~Oscar Levant

Standing at the cheery red front entrance, Harry Qualls couldn't believe Judith Webster hadn't rushed to open the door and snatch up the parcel he had for her. She usually peered through the curtains when she was expecting something. Ninety percent of the time she was friendly to him, except when she didn't get deliveries as soon as she'd hoped. She was harmless, but had one hell of a temper. He'd once seen her become so enraged by an invitation from her mother-in-law that she ran it through a paper shredder and set fire to it right on the brick porch.

He knocked once more, left the long package on the doorstep, and then whistled as he made his way down the street and back up the other side.

A Labrador retriever hiked his leg on the Webster's front porch to mark the spot, probably hoping to impress Gladys Neitz's toy poodle who was in heat next door. Harry crossed the street to shoo it away but he was too late, since he saw pee dripping down the package propped against the door. No way was he going to ring the doorbell to explain what happened, in case she tried to put the blame on him for being careless with her mail.

Heaven help that poor dog if Judith caught it.

It had taken all my remaining energy to change into the comfort of an old flannel nightgown when I got home yesterday afternoon. I fell into bed and stayed there most of the weekend. So depressed was I that even hearing the mailman knock on the door Saturday afternoon didn't rouse me from bed, where I pulled the covers up around my ears.

I'd spent the past twenty-four hours drifting through the bleakest recesses of my mind, a place much darker than my unlit bedroom. Every failure, both real and imagined, that I'd ever experienced loomed up to haunt me. Thoughts wouldn't quit invading my head, tormenting me with exaggerations of how boring my life was, how old I was getting, how ugly my appearance had become, and what a thoroughly useless human being I turned out to be. Everyone on the planet hated me, though I couldn't figure out exactly which of my faults pushed them to loath and ostracize me to this extent. Sleeping intermittently, I spent hours on end staring at a smudge on the bedroom wallpaper, a dirty fingerprint a few inches below the light switch, thinking about my fucked up existence.

My rambling brain sporadically turned to Evan Gallagher, lying near death on his oriental rug in Eldridge. Worried sick, I doubted anyone had found him and feared he must be in a great deal of pain after being shot, if he was still alive. I thought about dialing 911, except I didn't know where to send the ambulance. Apparently Eldridge was located in a very remote area, or it was possible that CIA agents patrolled the location to keep out terrorists and disgruntled fans. I wasn't sure which, but vaguely remembered seeing a news story confirming one or the other. I'd once attempted to send flowers to Martha Merriweather, hospitalized as she recovered from an experimental face lift, only to have the florist yell at me, saying he watched the same program and to lay off the practical jokes. What the fuck was his problem?

Overcome by loneliness, I wished my cat would've snuggled beside me the way she did on chilly nights. Miss Poopsie, however, was nowhere to be seen. The little bitch. When my dark moods hit, that selfish cat usually hid in a pile of clothes in the laundry room even though she knew I didn't spend much time in there.

When Greg came home that evening, he found me still lying in our dark bedroom. I hadn't budged from the spot he left me in that morning, nor had I gotten up to eat, piss, or even more unusual and disturbing, I hadn't yet staggered to the kitchen to siphon off a single drop from my schnapps collection.

"Honey," he said quietly, sitting down on the bed beside me. "Are you alright?"

"Everything's fine," I whispered. I had no intention of chasing off my husband, the only person who actually gave a damn about me, by regaling him with the details of all the horrible things that were wrong with me. If Greg had yet to figure out how stupid, ugly, and worthless I was, then too bad for him. I wasn't going to tell him. "I'm just tired . . . and in a bad mood." I pulled the covers up higher so they now obstructed all but the center of my face.

No matter what, I never questioned my love for my husband. Becoming Mrs. Gregory Webster sixteen years ago had truly been the best moment of my life. Whenever I got caught up in one of my celebrity crushes, they seemed to exist in a world parallel to the one Greg and I shared. My sometimes confused mind saw the two scenarios as separate concurrent entities. For example, if last year's crush on Henry Winkler—I went through a Fonzie phase around the time the cable channel ran a *Happy Days* marathon that summer—worked out so that I actually had moved into a house in Hawaii at the base of a volcano with him, I'd have expected Greg to be waiting in our Evansville home whenever I returned.

From past experience, he knew better than to push too hard when I was in one of these moods. If he continued to ask what was wrong or how I felt, he'd get his head bitten off before I shit it back out on his shoes. Hey, I have a right to be bitchy when I feel this bad, right? The best way for him to handle the situation is to act like every- thing is fine and go on about his business. I do not like to be doted on when I have one of my spells.

He walked to the closet. "You want me to fix you something to eat before I head out?" After sliding a few of the hangers across the rod, he found his lucky red and purple bowling shirt.

"No, not hungry."

"Want me to bring you some schnapps?" he asked as he changed clothes, using the same cheerful tone I sometimes use on Miss Poopsie.

"Nope."

"Well, I'm off to the big bowling tourna- ment." He gave me a peck on the blanket that covered my head before telling me goodbye, then turned in the bedroom doorway to ask, "Are you sure you're gonna be alright?"

In one swift motion, I sprang from being huddled under the sheet to a sitting position, my back ramrod straight. He should consider himself lucky my head didn't swivel around spewing green vomit.

"Goddamn it, Greg, I told you I was fine! What do you want me to do, you son of a bitch? Open a vein and write it in blood? I am just fuckin' peachy!" The last word was a high pitched screech that made him wince.

"Okay then." Greg plastered a weak excuse for a grin across his face and eased himself into the hall. "See you later, Judith."

He ducked in the nick of time. The box of tissues I threw at his head missed and bounced off the wall behind him. Fueled by the adrenaline my rage had brought, I jumped out of bed to follow him down the hall, bitching every step of the way. Why did he have to go and piss me off? Greg exited through the back door that led to the garage as I punctuated the end of my tirade by yelling a heartfelt "fuck you" at him.

My little hissy fit made me thirsty. I trudged to the kitchen and splashed a generous amount of butterscotch schnapps over the ice cubes I threw into the glass, the tallest I could find in the cupboard. Stomping back and forth across the living room, I nursed the schnappstail, wondering what kind of sadistic thrill Greg got from pushing my buttons like that. I refilled the empty glass and hoped he was happy with himself.

After pacing a few miles inside my home, I was again repeating the circuit through the living room, hall, and, when turning a sharp pivot as I reached the back wall in the computer room, suddenly remembered something very important. I seemed to recall a knock on the door that afternoon while I laid in bed like a vegetable.

I marched through my living room once

more and placed the schnapps on a coaster. In the foyer, I paused to flip on the porch light and turned the decorative bronze knob on the front door. Breath held, desperately not wanting to get my hopes up only to have them thwarted, I pulled the door open.

"It came! It came!" I hugged the parcel I'd found beside the doorstep to my chest. "Of all days, it finally fuckin' came!"

Too excited to waste time going after a knife, I tore into the cardboard box with my bare hands, breaking two nails in the process. When the hole was large enough, I reached into the package. Performing what looked like a cesarean section on my rectangular patient, I pulled out the object I'd been waiting for these last long weeks.

I finally held my very own shillelagh in my hands!

After staring at it for some time, I gently placed the traditional Irish fighting club, hand crafted from the finest blackthorn wood ever grown on the Emerald Isle, on the coffee table to better admire it. Leaning forward with my elbows on my knees, chin in my upturned palms, one hand on each cheek, I gazed at the long awaited treasure. My nose began to twitch like a bunny rabbit's and a strange acrid smell distracted me from my daydreams.

My attention turned to the shillelagh's ravaged container, which I decided to check to see if instructions had been included. The odor grew stronger while I sifted through bits of Styrofoam and wads of crumpled newspaper used as packing material, dropping them carelessly to the floor as I went.

"Eeew." I rubbed my fingertips with my thumbs since my hands seemed to be coated with some sticky, gummy substance.

I sniffed my fingers, scrunching my face in disgust at the oddly familiar odor. What the hell was it, rancid peanut butter maybe? Upon closer inspection of the box I'd been handling, I found a large yellowish stain splattered all down one side. Some of the packing material on the floor also looked as if it'd come in contact with the contaminant.

"Goddamn it," I said flatly, my nose right on the stench when I realized what the stuff had to be. Urine. "Harry Qualls, you son of a bitch!"

Harry had waited until a day he knew I was lying in bed, too depressed to answer the door, before he finally decided to deliver the package. In my mind, I could see short, skinny-assed Harry sneak onto the porch with his big mailman purse slung over his shoulder, looking to the left, then to the right to make sure none of the nosey neighbors like Gladys Neitz saw what he planned to do. I could almost hear his sadistic laughter as he set the cardboard box addressed to me in front of the door, then unzipped his pants and pulled out his scrawny inch-long nubbin of a pecker. He would've leaned against my nicely painted red door frame and probably whistled one of his damn moronic tunes as he pissed all over my package, shaking his minuscule penis like a miniature fire hose. I could just picture him, a maniacal grin beneath his stupid looking mustache, his smartass voice saying, "And piss on you too, *Judy*!"

I sprayed the new shillelagh down with Lysol to kill Harry's nasty urine germs, then with Febreze to cover the hospital-like pine scent with a flowery fragrance. I did a quick visual inspection to make sure there were no piss stains on the fine blackthorn wood.

Then I saw it.

There, on the underside of the weighted knob, a nick the size and shape of a grain of rice. No one else would notice the tiny imperfection, but to me, it may as well have been a huge purple paint splotch. The room spun around me like an evil tilt-a-whirl gone out of control until my head nearly exploded.

"You've done it now, Harry, you stupid little motherfucker!" I raged. "How dare you break my stuff!"

I refilled my drink, then took up pacing

around the house again. "I *so* wish lepre-chauns were real so I could send one to fuck you in the ass!"

I finally settled down around one o'clock in the morning. Exhausted, the depression washed over me again, leaving me drained and broken. Tears slid down my face when I glanced at the shillelagh. Why did every-thing I love have to get fucked up?

Shillelagh in hand, I moped down the hall to bed.

One thing, at least, comforted me. I'd al-ready added Mr. Harry Qualls' name to my shit list. Good thing, since I was too spent to go through the trouble of retrieving it from its hiding place. I couldn't wait to let him have it.

When Greg got home a short time later, a second place bowling trophy carried proudly under his arm, he knew Judith was still in a bad mood. Cardboard and

Styrofoam littered the living room again, and he didn't even want to know what smelled like piss. At least there was no broken glass, and the remote was still in one piece.

Cleaning up the mess, Greg hoped his wife would get over this spell of depression soon. Lord help him if he had to take her back to that psychiatrist. For the most part, he thought shrinks were full of shit, though he would've liked to have some more of the pills they'd prescribed for her, the green ones that helped even out her moods in times like these so she could get out of bed, but without the violent screaming fits.

Other than the meds, he had very little confidence in the psychiatrists. Over the years, they hadn't been able to find a diagnosis to fit Judith that their expert team agreed on. Though most had used the words bipolar and manic depressive, they'd also thrown around terms like obsessive compulsive, attention deficit disorder, borderline personality—whatever the hell that meant, he never quite understood—and schizophrenia. The latter was usually ruled out due to the fact that Judith didn't hear voices in her head, or if she did, she never admitted it. They couldn't make up their minds about what was wrong with her. Greg thought she was basically a little overly sensitive and prone to mood swings.

He popped open a beer and gave the cat a scratch behind the ears, then settled on the couch to watch a late-night movie before falling asleep. Both he and Miss Poopsie had better judgment than to go to bed and risk Judith's wrath, should they accidentally wake her up.

Chapter Eight

*No excellent soul is exempt from a
mixture of madness.*
~Aristotle

I spent Sunday in bed, buried under the
covers with the shades pulled down. My
mind tormented me with all my failings and
shortcomings, all the dreams I never
reached, all the things I'd never have. It
would've been nice to have a son or daughter to keep me company, but I'd just have to
settle for a cat too selfish to spare even a
couple measly purrs on a day I felt so shitty. A foster kid would've been nice, but that

didn't happen since that Fulkerson asshole blocked the parking spaces at the rental place so I couldn't pick up a leaf blower to dry the stupid carpet I'd shampooed before the case worker came for the home visit. The wet carpet had to be the only reason that snooty bitch denied my application. I would've been a damn fine foster mom, but no. Why do people always screw me over?

The shillelagh lay on the pillow beside me. After staring at it a few hours, my attention turned to the book I'd bought from Amazon. At least Harry delivered that without pissing all over it. I gathered the energy to sit up and took the book in its place of honor on the nightstand. Mostly I looked at the beautifully painted pictures as I turned the pages, particularly liking the ones that depicted Irishmen sparring, wielding their Shillelaghs as if their life and country depended on them knocking some sense into their enemies. I was also drawn to the sketch of a wee leprechaun, comically brandishing his weapon at a peasant who tried to steal his gold. I was still pretty disappointed those things weren't real.

Greg poked his head in the room to check on me. Absentmindedly sliding the locket that held Evan's picture along my necklace, I was reading an interesting page about the proper way to crack a skull without spilling a single drop of blood.

A few hours later, however, when he looked back in, I lay huddled beneath the sheets again. "Hey, you know what would be fun? We could get on eBay and buy some new cocktail glasses, or maybe a new collar for Miss Poopsie." Greg smiled at me when I flopped over to look at him. "Come on, what do you say?"

"We probably wouldn't win the bid, anyway." I sighed. "Just piss on it."

Then I broke into hysterical laughter.

"Okay then, maybe we'll try it tomorrow." He didn't understand what was so funny, but he didn't press his luck, probably afraid I'd throw something else at him if he kept talking so much. He went outside to spend the sunny but cool November afternoon cleaning leaves out of the gutters.

The blues still weighed heavily on me Monday, though I did manage to haul my ass to the living room recliner in time for the opening credits of *Heartbeats and Teardrops*. No matter how shitty I felt, I had to find out whether poor Evan Gallagher was alive or dead.

Waiting for the soap to start, I tried to think up a good excuse to give my boss at the Gas 'N Go since I planned to call in sick when my program went off. If I felt too bad to pour myself a drink, I had no business waiting on a convenience store full of assholes. "To hell with the fuckers." I clicked up the volume with the remote as my show started.

Screaming sirens announced the paramedics' arrival after a maid who'd heard the gunshot called 911. "He's still alive!" exclaimed an EMT holding Evan's wrist when he found a pulse. They loaded the patient in the ambulance and whisked him off to the hospital, red lights flashing.

He was alive! That news lifted the black veil of desperation off me. During the first commercial break, I managed to lift my butt out of the recliner, poured spearmint schnapps to celebrate, and took my seat as a deodorant advertisement ended.

I nibbled M&Ms from the crystal candy dish—one of last year's eBay specials—as I watched the next scene. The M&Ms mingled deliciously with the ice cold schnapps and reminded me of mint chocolate chip ice cream. My stomach welcomed the food since I'd hardly eaten anything the past weekend.

On the TV, Dr. Melinda Martin had just listened to the still hypnotized Cynthia DeHaven name Blake Carmichael as her baby's daddy. Having ignored a pass made by him at the sleazy bar two months back, Blake must've slipped her a drug that totally wiped away all memory of the steamy night they spent knocking boots under the pool table in the back of the bar.

The camera broke to a segment on Evan Gallagher. He was admitted through the emergency room, paramedics scurrying beside his gurney in a tangle of IV bags. The doctor on duty yelled for his staff to prepare the operating room. What I wouldn't give to be at the hospital and hold his hand in this, his hour of need. A close-up of Evan's unconscious but still handsome face was the last thing they showed before cheesy music started playing, signaling another short break for a word from their sponsors.

The soap opera returned to the psychiatrist's office. I took a big swig of spearmint schnapps and anticipated a juicy scene as I set the glass on the coaster by the empty candy dish. The segment revealed Dr. Martin's secret agenda. She was one of the college girls Cynthia had a lesbian affair with years ago during her 'experimental stage'. Due to a fifty pound weight loss, an expensive nose job, and the fact that she'd changed her first name from Muffy to Melinda, Cynthia hadn't recognized her old lover, the girl she'd jilted on that long ago Valentine's Day. Before bringing her out of hypnosis, Melinda vowed to make her pay, and pay dearly.

Scenes from the next episode didn't reveal much. Martha Merriweather and her two grown children, James and Vivian, schemed to further injure heartthrob Evan Gallagher when and if he made it through surgery to remove the bullet James had shot him with. Dr. Melinda Martin was shown meandering around, following the unsuspecting and very pregnant Cynthia DeHaven through town.

I daydreamed, sliding my locket along its chain as the narrator's voice ended the show with the familiar line, ". . . tune in tomorrow for more *Heartbeats and Teardrops*."

I didn't call in sick after all. I felt much better after seeing Evan alive in the hospital and felt like I could muster up and go on in to work.

At the Gas 'N Go that night, I was surprised to see my bitchy boss waiting to speak with me. The words 'whoop tee doo' echoed through my head, but I made a conscious effort not to say it out loud. I hated her almost as much as I hated my stupid job.

I didn't have to wait long to find out what Susan wanted. Some of last week's sales didn't jibe with the inventory, and there was the matter of Friday afternoon's surveillance tape. She got right to the point, asking me why they were coming up short on potato chips, candy bars, and other odds and ends.

"You know," I said, tapping an index finger against my chin to help me think, "there have been a few people in here that I kind of suspected of shoplifting. They were good at it, though, since I didn't see anything I could use to *prove* they were stealing."

"So, why didn't you stop them," asked Susan, looking skeptical. God, she's such a bitch.

"You've got to be kidding," I replied, laughing. "You people don't pay me enough to wrestle candy bars away from petty criminals. Do I look like Dog the Bounty Hunter, for Christ's sakc?"

I was no fool. Whenever I helped myself to a snack, I made sure to either do it off camera or with my back to the lens acting like I was cleaning something. Frank and every other employee there took those freebies, so it wasn't a big deal. Nobody could prove I did anything wrong. So, there I sat, the epitome of innocence.

By the way Susan stared at me, it was obvious she was too stupid to see the humor in the situation. After yammering on a while about the proper protocol to follow with future shoplifters, she moved on to the next issue.

On the store room monitor she played Friday's security footage for me. Susan wanted to know why I felt the need to run to the bathroom and stay there for fifteen minutes while a store full of customers packed the place off.

"So Judy, explain to me why you left the register unattended."

"First of all, my name is *Judith*, not Judy. I think we've talked about that before, haven't we?" I asked, straining to sound sweet and look calm. Susan knew I hated being called by that nickname and was just trying to get a rise out of me, but I wasn't about to give the bitch the satisfaction.

"Yes, sorry then, *Judith*," Susan said, pronouncing my name like it was the glow-in-the-dark clap. "Please, go on with your explanation."

"Well, you see," I explained, "I was sick. I think having to come in on day shift really messed my system up. Matter of fact, I was sick in bed all weekend. You can call and ask my husband about it, if you want." I was the vision of sincerity as I spoke, plus the depression had taken its toll on me. I'd noticed how pale and haggard my face was when I put on makeup that afternoon.

"You do look sort of puny." Susan blew out an exasperated sigh. "Go on."

"You can see on the film that I was drinking my orange juice, hoping it would settle my stomach. I took it with me when I had to go to the ladies' room. See," I said, pointing to the image of me, frozen on the monitor, carrying a fuzzy armload as I left the counter. "And I even took paperwork with me, so I wouldn't waste time while I was in there."

Susan looked at the blurred images on the screen and couldn't tell for certain what I'd been carrying. "But why did you have to go when the store was full and stay so long? What in the world were you doing in there for fifteen minutes?" Susan asked, a sanctimonious sneer smeared across her stupid face.

"It just hit me all of a sudden. You see, I

had diarrhea and an upset stomach at the same time, so it took me a while to get everything worked out. When you've got to go, you've got to go."

"Well, next time, at least wait until the customers empty out before you go running off to the toilet, sick or not." Susan's smartass tone made me want to slap the glasses off her head.

"Okay," I replied innocently, a naive expression plastered on my face. "But won't it violate a health code if I puke on the merchandise and splatter my diarrhea shit all over the customers?"

Bingo! I'd made a point she couldn't argue with. Susan stood speechless and turned purple before she stormed out of the Gas 'N Go. I celebrated winning that disagreement with another OJ's glove.

Chapter Nine

*I can calculate the motion of heavenly bodies
but not the madness of people.*
~Sir Isaac Newton

Outside the living room window, a graceful swirl of brown and gold leaves danced in the crisp autumn air. Trees lining the street were mostly bare now, the stormy weather having stripped the foliage earlier than I would've liked. I waited for the mailman to come striding through the flurry of leaves.

Stirring root beer schnapps into a mug of root beer with one of my blown glass swizzle sticks, I thought about adding a nice big scoop of ice cream. Then I spotted Harry walking up the street in the direction of my house, whistling the tune to *Bonanza* as he delivered envelopes into letter boxes and through mail slots.

I opened the door just as he reached my porch. My face was a serene mask of polite calmness, disguising the anger that burned in my gut over the mail carrier's prior acts of disrespect. A warm smile appeared beneath Harry's mustache when he saw me getting ready to greet him at my entryway. The bastard probably wished it was snowing so he could've asked me for a steaming cup of cocoa on this nippy afternoon.

I quickly ushered him inside and shut the door behind us.

"I have a letter to mail, but I need some help with it," I said, limping a bit as I led him toward the dining room. "I put a stamp on it and had it all ready for you, but then the silly cat knocked it off the table. You know how Miss Poopsie is, always trying to take over the furniture. I think it went up under the china cabinet." I pointed at the corner of a white envelope, barely visible behind the ornate legs of the hutch that held my wedding china and a few nice pieces of crystal.

"Could you please be a dear and get it out for me?" I tried my best to sound like a demure lady in distress. "I hate to ask, but the arthritis in my knee is acting up, what with the cool turn in the weather. Anyway, if I got down on the floor, I'd have the devil of a time getting back up."

"No problem at all, Mrs. Webster," Harry said cheerfully, already dropping to his knees to retrieve the fallen envelope. He put his right hand under the hutch and felt around for the letter.

"I think you're just about to get it, Harry," I said, right before I clocked him on the head.

The shillelagh handled like a dream. Held with my thumb pointing toward the knob end, as per the instructions in *Martial Arts of the Irishman*, I brought it down a second and third time against the mailman's temple. The first blow had been a swift upswing that kissed the base of his skull, successfully knocking him out. The consecutive licks were meant to finish him off.

Poor Harry Qualls never knew what hit him. I'd carried the shillelagh like a cane, which fit perfectly with my fake limp and the story about my bum knee. If I ever did develop arthritis, the massive amount of schnapps in my bloodstream would kill the pain long before I ever felt it.

With my hand on my hip and a smirk of satisfaction on my face, I rolled ole Harry over on his back and poked him with the shillelagh a few times. He was dead alright. Just to be on the safe side, I put a plastic garbage bag over his head and secured it in place with a long piece of string tied in a pretty bow situated over his Adam's apple.

"Well, Harry, I guess this teaches you a lesson for pissing on my packages, huh!"

On the off chance he wasn't already

good and dead, the plastic bag would suffocate him in a matter of minutes. To kill time, I decided to take myself up on the idea about the float. Humming the theme to *Rocky*, I whipped up a root beer and schnapps float topped with a huge scoop of fudge marble ice cream. I enjoyed my snack at the dining room table, glad I'd recorded today's episode of *Heartbeats and Teardrops*. Wouldn't want to spoil a perfect day like this by missing my Evan fix.

As I drained my schnapps float, I took the opportunity to look through Harry's big mailman purse. I'd always wanted to look inside it and this was my chance. I didn't find anything but a bunch of letters, no hair brush or personal effects of any kind. The only thing to pique my interest was a package the size of a deck of playing cards addressed to Gladys Neitz next door. It was ethically wrong and some sort of federal crime to open other people's mail. That would've been wrong and I, Judith Webster, always played by the rules. I reluctantly dropped it back in the pouch with all the boring letters and junk mail.

I licked the last drop of ice cream from the spoon before going to retrieve a compact from my purse, then removed the bag from my mailman's head. Unable to find a pulse, I put the compact in front of his nose and mouth to make sure he wasn't breathing. The mirror didn't fog up, so I counted this as a job well done.

On to the business of getting rid of him. The garbage truck was due to pass by in a couple of hours so I planned to have what was left of ole Harry Qualls all packed up and waiting on the curb by then.

Luckily, there was no blood to clean up. The molten lead in the knob end of the Irish fighting club had done a wonderful job of beating the life out of him without making any cuts, only a cluster of goose eggs. I was really relieved as I inspected his head, since the sight of blood always made me queasy. Apparently, bruises didn't form on a dead person's skin the same way they did on a live one's, since Harry's temple was only slightly discolored.

Due to Qualls' stature, I found it easier than anticipated to stuff his short body into a large Hefty bag. I tossed his mailman purse in, which came to rest on his midsection. I double bagged him just to make sure the thick plastic wouldn't rip on the way to the curb. Didn't want to waste time packaging him up all over again.

"Hmmmmmm." Something didn't look just right. I thought on it a moment before running to the bathroom. I returned shortly with Miss Poopsie's litter box and an economy pack of generic tampons, then grabbed a bottle of ketchup from the fridge and a ceramic mixing bowl. The bag wasn't full enough so I dumped the used cat litter over the body. Considering the fact Harry loved to piss on stuff, he ought to enjoy passing into the afterlife surrounded by urine soaked pebbles and cat turds.

My craft project had the right shape and felt like normal garbage now, in case anyone put their hands on it. For the next order of business, I opened the tampons and removed their slim pink applicators. As I poured half the bottle of tomato ketchup into the green ceramic bowl, I knew I was a genius. After I finished with Harry, I'd make a note in my journal to take the Mensa test.

Even though Harry had turned out to be a real asshole in life, he had been a living creature, after all, and was entitled to some dignity in his burial in the landfill or wherever the hell the garbage truck took him. I didn't want any homeless people desecrating my mailman's body by rifling through his Hefty shroud. My plan would do the trick to deter even the most desperate of destitutes.

Giggling at both my brilliant idea and the oddness of what I was doing, I plunged each tampon deep into the ketchup and let them soak a few minutes, since they'd look more authentic if they swelled open. The green bowl really did look kind of cool. With the string end of the feminine hygiene products sticking out of the red condiment, it looked just like some bizarre mutation of a tropical flower. When they'd set long enough, I threw them into the garbage sack, arranging them so they were evenly distributed around all sides of the body. Now he could go on to his final resting place with dignity.

"That should do it for you, Harry." If anyone peeked inside the bag, they'd think it was full of ordinary bathroom refuse. Vagrants would surely leave it alone as soon as they smelled the dirty kitty litter, and my artistically decorated generic tampons should keep anyone with half a brain from sticking their hands inside. Satisfied with my ingenuity, I fastened the bag with a couple of the yellow twisty things that came in the Hefty box.

The last step was to get Harry's carcass out to the curb in time for pick up. Although he couldn't have weighed more than a hundred and fifty pounds sopping wet, I couldn't sling the full Hefty bag over my shoulder and stroll outside like I'd planned. Not to worry, though, because my little red wagon was out in the garage. I normally used it for the Christmas display I set up in the front yard every December, but it would make a cool taxi for my very dead mailman.

It took some effort, but after much heaving, pushing, and maneuvering, I had the bag-o-corpse loaded onto the little red wagon, its cute whitewall wheels ready and waiting to take their dearly departed passenger on his last bumpy ride. In no time at all, there was a tidy garbage bag setting on the curb. I took out the kitchen trash as well, thinking more garbage would seem less conspicuous.

I made a fuzzy navel to celebrate, loving how the peach schnapps tasted with my fresh-from-the-can orange juice. Pulling on a jacket, I went to sit on the front porch to drink it. When the city workers loaded the garbage bags into the trash compactor on the back of their truck, I waved at them and told them to have a nice day. Fall is such a beautiful time of year.

Chapter Ten

Sanity is very rare: every man almost,
and every woman, has a dash of madness.
~Ralph Waldo Emerson

As I perused the schnapps section at Corkers, I noticed a fresh new face behind the counter. The pretty dark-haired girl seemed much more pleasant than the grouchy old cigar smoking goober she'd replaced.

Arms loaded down with bottles of schnapps, I walked up front to check out.

"Oh, these look yummy." I read the name Lori McClanahan on the clerk's name tag as she rang up my merchandise. "I had no idea you could get this stuff in such cool flavors."

"Schnapps comes in thirty-four flavors," I said, proud of my knowledge on such important alcohol trivia. "Most of them are pretty good." So far, I'd thoroughly enjoyed all but the cranberry flavor. That one I didn't care for, but thought it might spice up the cranberry sauce I always took to Greg's mom's house on Thanksgiving and Christmas.

"How about this one," Lori asked, pausing before she bagged the last bottle. "What the hell does a pomegranate taste like, anyway?"

"Don't know yet, this is the first time I've bought that flavor." I knew I was going to like this woman. Anybody who took an interest in the finer points of schnapps was okay in my book. "The caramel apple is one of my favorites, though. Tastes great in an apple martini. Much better than apple pucker."

Lori handed me the change and flashed a warm smile. "I'll have to try it sometime. Let me know how the other one turns out."

I detected a New York accent in the husky voice that seemed to fit Lori's personality. She surprised me by adding a free store sample of rum to my bag.

I was already beginning to think of her as my new best friend. With a name like McClanahan, she had to come from a nice Irish family.

Later that day my schnapps level made the purple memo pad kind of hard to locate, but at last I found it tucked underneath my sofa cushion. I jotted down as much information as I could before the commercial ended, careful to get the website address correct. This was the first time I'd seen this event advertised on SoapNet. I had to get the facts straight so I could make plans.

The cast of *Heartbeats and Teardrops*

would have a Meet and Greet for their loyal following of soap fans, the venue a fancy hotel in Nashville. I couldn't believe I was actually going to see them up close! Evan Gallagher and I were destined to meet and marry, but this was so much quicker than I'd imagined.

I made a Drunken Leprechaun to celebrate the exciting news and drank the schnappstail as I daydreamed. I pictured myself as the line in front of me waiting to greet Evan Gallagher grew ever shorter. I'd will myself to stay calm when my turn finally came, then introduce myself with a handshake, gazing at him through a flutter of lashes and a coy smile. Evan would look into my eyes, instantly recognize his soul mate, and pull me into his strong Irish arms in a hug that would surely embarrass the throng of onlookers. He'd probably want to leave the Meet and Greet with me immediately, but the show's producers would make him wait until he addressed the rest of the people in line. Fine with me, since I didn't want to get my future husband fired. Evan would insist on signing the remaining autographs with me sitting on his lap, unable to bear the absence of my loving touch for even a few short moments.

The empty glass beckoned me back to the present, temporarily putting my romantic plans on hold while I went to make another drink.

Reclaiming my seat on the couch with a newly refreshed Guinness and caramel apple schnappstail, I pulled the phone into my lap and dialed the number to Susan's office. Better to let her know as soon as possible that I'd need that day off. As it started to ring, I tried to formulate a valid sounding excuse. Luckily, the perfect one popped into my head before she answered and I told her which day I couldn't work.

"Yeah, I have to drive my cat, Miss Poopsie, to Nashville for a veterinary appointment."

"Why do you have to drive two hours when there's a perfectly good vet clinic right down the street from the Gas 'N Go?" Susan asked in her usual hateful tone, and then sighed. "I'm getting a headache."

"Well, Miss Poopsie needs gall bladder surgery and Dr. Gallagher is a specialist in the field of feline innards." I struggled to restrain myself from telling her what I really thought about her and that stupid c-store job. Bitch better watch it or she'd find her ass on my shit list. "The procedure's going to be risky, since she's a hemophiliac."

"You really expect me to believe—" She exhaled a melodramatic sigh into the receiver. "Fine, get your cat a bikini wax while you're there, for all I care. My head's pounding and I don't have time to deal with this nonsense." She must've hung up on me then because the dial tone hummed in my ear. God, she really was a moron, thinking Miss Poopsie would sit still for a wax job when the cat wouldn't even let me pluck her whiskers. I put the phone down and prayed for Susan to have an aneurysm.

With that business all settled, I spent

the next few hours at the computer. First looking up the website that contained all the information on the upcoming Meet and Greet, then shopping for emerald green dresses on eBay.

The impending Nashville trip triggered a bout of insomnia, and I turned into a ball of energy. Barely able to sleep two hours a night, my eyelids would spring open long before daylight, my mind reeling with all the stuff I needed to do.

My daily routine was totally different than it used to be, my sudden interest in physical fitness being the most radical change. I needed to firm up my flabby ass before I met Evan Gallagher, the man I was destined to marry, so I made an emergency two a.m. trip to Walmart to buy a half dozen exercise DVDs. Miss Poopsie had no idea what to think when, hell bent on shaping up, I spent hours at a time gyrating around the living room to various video gurus. The kickboxing one was the noisiest, but the cat found the weird Yoga postures the most disturbing, I think, since she'd stalk out of the room. After my cool down, I'd munch on Lucky Charms and wash them down with a health tonic of grape juice and butterscotch schnapps.

Shillelagh practice filled the afternoons while I waited for *Heartbeats and Teardrops* to come on. I reread the training manual over and over, and felt empowered while practicing the ancient Irish self-defense techniques.

Cleaning was my new hobby, and I fixated on odd areas around the house. Our doorknobs were all polished after getting sterilized with bleach. I organized the kitchen cupboards, the utensils housed therein lined up according to size, shape, and how much schnapps they could hold. Every pair of underwear in the house had been ironed before I placed them back inside their drawer, a shiny layer of tinfoil now lining the bottom.

Miss Poopsie certainly didn't seem to enjoy her bubble bath, but I knew she appreciated the catnip-filled mice I put inside her fancy goldfish bed. No matter how busy I was, I made sure to take time to let the kitty play inside it at least an hour a day. The mice were on sale at the pet store, originally intended to become snake food. I couldn't stand to let them fall to that barbaric fate so I put them in a Ziploc bag in the freezer until they passed on peacefully, then stuffed them with catnip and sewed their little bellies back up with festive pink thread. They could be left out at room temperature for two whole days before they started to stink.

The shamrock green paint on sale at Home Depot gave me the urge to redecorate. Imagine Greg's surprise when he came home one afternoon to discover one wall in each room of the house turned the color of a ripe lime.

Most of the time my thoughts, when

reined in, focused on the new love of my life, Evan. I filled an entire journal with scribblings in his honor. The front page boasted a heart doodle pierced by Cupid's arrow, 'Judith loves Evan' neatly penned in the center. Next came dozens of sheets with 'Evan Gallagher' taking up every centimeter of white space, front and back. The rest of the journal pages were full of 'Mrs. Judith Ann Gallagher', sporadically interspersed with 'Evan and Judith, True Love 4 Ever'. On the last page, I'd tried to draw a leprechaun shooting hearts from his shillelagh, but, unhappy with the result, I colored over it with a green gel pen, transforming it into a giant shamrock.

A trip to the local library scored three Irish cookbooks. I studied the recipes, trying to decide which meals my new husband would like best. The stew was too complicated, and since I planned on spending more time in the bedroom with Evan than slaving away in the kitchen, I decided to concentrate on something easier. Soda bread seemed doable, as did the cabbage concoction on page forty-seven of *Top Irish Recipes*. Potato candy sounded delicious, yet quick to make, while the Irish coffee was right up my alley.

After *Heartbeats and Teardrops* went off, I thought about my new best friend, Lori. She was probably at work, so I searched through an old telephone book for the number to Corkers Liquor Store, then dialed it as I sipped on a cold glass of blueberry schnapps.

It suddenly occurred to me that I should have some kind of business related reason to call her place of employment, just in case her boss overheard part of the conversation. I didn't want to get my BFF in trouble, after all.

"Hi, this is Judith. I was wondering if you had any new types of schnapps in? I heard they were coming out with a peanut butter flavor." I really hadn't, but that would be one hell of a delicious taste sensation.

"Don't think so, but let me check the computer for you." After a query on the PC in front of her, no peanut butter schnapps appeared on the inventory. "Sorry, but we don't have that. I remember you, though, the schnapps aficionado. How ya doing?"

"Oh, pretty good." Of course my buddy remembered me. Duh. "I'm planning a trip to Nashville in a couple of days. Been looking forward to it." I filled her in on the details about the Meet and Greet, hoping she'd ask to tag along.

"Ya know, I never really got into the whole soap thing. The plots just seem too cornball to me," Lori said. "But I hope you have a fun trip."

What the hell did she say? How could anybody not like the soaps?

To end the conversation on a positive note, I changed the subject. "Well, I'll have to get off here soon to get to Willard Library before they close, to research my family tree. My O'Malley line goes all the way back to County Cork," I lied. I didn't even know my grandmother's maiden name, nor did I have the slightest interest in such crap. I wanted to make a good impression with what I believed to be a common interest. "You're Irish, right?"

"You better not let my grandpa hear you say that!" Lori had the audacity to laugh. "We're of the Clan McClanahan, from the Scottish highlands. Gramps was born and raised there. Afraid he doesn't think too highly of the Irish. He told me stories about—"

"Somebody's at the door. Gotta go." I slammed the phone down, stunned over what I'd just heard. "What a fuckin' bitch!" I said to Miss Poopsie, who was currently sulking inside the confines of her goldfish bed, the entrance having been taped shut again, imprisoning her inside for her en-joyment.

"You think you know somebody." I

headed for the kitchen and my booze stash. "Not only does that little whore Lori *not* watch the soaps, she hates Irish people! Aaaaggh!" I made myself a stiff schnappstail and paced around the house like a caged panther on speed.

My pulse raced as my anger grew. How dare that little bitch lie to me like this? McClanahan sounded like a nice Irish name, but no, she was actually a racist Scottish bitch who thought she was better than Evan's family because her stupid cocksucking grandpa was born in the Scotch highlands, of all places. Well, la-tee-fucking-dah.

"I'll show her, all right." I'd make Lori very sorry she and her prejudiced grand-parents had been ever born.

Chapter Eleven

When we remember that we are all mad,
the mysteries disappear and life
stands explained.
~Mark Twain

Tally notes in my left hand, a drink in my right, I watched the roulette wheel spin to a halt. "Thirteen" from the dealer confirmed that I'd lost yet another round, along with my twenty-five dollar wager.

Realizing the next spin of the wheel would be my last bet of the night, I made the thirty-third tally mark on the small scrap of folded paper I kept hidden under my hand. I whispered my poem as I put chips on the corresponding numbers. "Seven and eleven, take me to heaven. Nineteen, I'm an Irish queen. Twenty-one, let's have us some fun. Thirty-four, a winner for sure. And Lori's a whore!"

The older gentleman a few seats away sent a pointed glance first at me, then my cup. "Haven't you drank your limit on those yet?"

I was only on my sixth drink of the evening, so I was nowhere near my limit. The old guy must be trying to pick me up. "Not by a long shot, but I'm a happily married woman so no, you cannot buy me a drink."

The old fart's feelings must've been hurt because he looked at me like I was out of my mind to turn him down.

While the little ball skipped around the wheel, Lori invaded my thoughts again. I'd called my best friend in all the world hoping she'd want to go to the *Heartbeats and Teardrops* Meet and Greet with me. Instead of being able to introduce her to my new fiancé, I was rudely forced to see her true colors. The Irish-hating Scottish bitch didn't even have the good sense to like the soaps! Lori was too damn stupid to be alive.

The dealer announced double zero, which made all but one of the roulette players sitting and standing around the table groan.

"Well, that's just goddamn great!" I'd used up my thirty-third bet along with all the cash I brought to gamble with. Realizing I'd been thinking about my new enemy as the ball landed on green made me see red. I shoved the tally sheet and little pencil into my purse as I stomped toward the parking lot, wielding the shillelagh as a walking stick.

McClanahan sounded like an Irish name to me, but no, it was Scottish. My losing streak tonight had to be due to a jinx Lori put on me. The double zero hardly ever came up, so I pictured Lori and her asinine grandpa laughing about how they'd rigged the game. Since they hated the Irish family I would join when I married Evan, they'd chosen the green space on the wheel to make me hate green, the color of the shamrock and all that symbolized Ireland! I could just see Grandpa McClanahan pissing his Depends, overcome with hysterical laughter when his granddaughter drew a mustache on one of Evan's glossy autographed photos before blackening in his perfect teeth.

I slammed the car door and cranked the ignition. "You'll pay for this one, *Lori!*" I yelled, drawing out her name in long venom-coated syllables. My tires squealed on to the highway as I formulated a plan. By the time I pulled into my driveway, I'd worked out the details for getting rid of the bitch. I staggered into the house and scrawled Lori's name on my shit list.

The following morning, I started preparations. I cleaned and polished Greg's old pistol until some of the finish came off. I selected six of the most perfect, flawless bullets from their small box and lined them up in a neat row on the kitchen table in front of the gleaming Smith and Wesson. One by one, I dipped the tip of each lethal projectile into a shot glass filled with hot sauce, careful not to immerse them too deeply for fear the gunpowder contained in the flat ends would get damp and screw up my plan. Humming the theme song to my soap opera, I took the bullets out to the backyard, arranged them standing on their ends on an old newspaper, and painted them with some of the leftover shamrock green paint I'd recently used on the walls. Next, I blew them dry with a hairdryer. Satisfied that they were dry and ready for killing, I loaded them into the revolving chamber.

I tucked the gun in to my favorite black purse. All I had to do now was wait until the time was right, to find the opportune moment when Lori was at work by herself with no customers in the liquor store, then **BOOM**! The bitch would never again disrespect Ireland, Judith Ann Webster, or my beloved soap opera.

That out of the way, I savored three schnappstails during *Heartbeats and Teardrops* as Miss Poopsie enjoyed her mandatory playtime taped inside her goldfish bed. Greg was working a double shift so I wouldn't see him again until the evening following my big Nashville trip.

I sat glued to the TV during this episode, hoping the actors would mention something about the Meet and Greet. I could hardly believe it was all happening the next day. I was finally going to meet Evan Gallagher, the man I was destined to marry, have him fall madly in love with me, and possibly even propose in front of a room full of adoring fans. Maybe one of the bystanders would offer to throw us an impromptu shower before we eloped.

That just wasn't realistic at all.

Evan's half-sister, Sylvia Carmichael, would obviously want that honor for herself.

That night, I carefully laid out the outfit I planned to wear the next day, a gorgeous emerald green wrap dress with strappy black pumps. Since I didn't have to work, I spent the evening going over the map and driving directions. I'd been to Nashville plenty of times but wanted to make sure I didn't accidentally make any wrong turns. It was a two-hour drive from my house and I hoped to arrive at the hotel for the Meet and Greet a few hours early.

So excited was I that sleep eluded me after I tucked myself into bed. I stared at the ceiling for over an hour, then, noticing the time on the alarm clock, realized I had to do something. If I didn't get enough beauty rest, I'd look like shit the next day when I met Evan, and that just wouldn't do.

A trip to the bathroom medicine cabinet produced two blue sleeping pills that I washed down with a few gulps of peppermint schnapps. I reread the dosage directions on the back of the bottle and decided that if it recommended two pills, I might ought to be on the safe side and take three extra. As the five pills mixed with the alcohol in my stomach, I snuggled under the covers and was fast asleep within half an hour.

"No!"

I couldn't believe my groggy, horrified eyes. The clock read twelve minutes past four o'clock . . . in the afternoon. The Meet and Greet would start in less than an hour. There was no possible way I could make it there in time to see my beloved Evan.

"Goddamn it to hell!"

Banging my head into the door frame for the sixth time, I wailed, "Why am I so fucking stupid?" I slid to the floor in an anguished heap.

Why had I slept so late? Sleeping pills didn't usually have that effect on me. My desperation turned to rage. The pills. I'd bought them at the pharmacy next door to Corkers.

"Oh, wait until I get my hands on you,

you fucking bitch!" I screeched, the last few words so high pitched that dogs down the street began to howl.

Thoughts tumbled through my brain. Lori tampered with the bottle of over-the-counter tranquilizers while they were still on the store shelf. Somehow, she must have known I'd buy that particular bottle for Greg, who sometimes had trouble sleeping.

But why? There were only two possibilities. The first was that Lori wanted to kill Greg because she was jealous of our blissful marriage. The second was that she'd somehow foreseen that her best friend, me, would have trouble sleeping on the eve of the Meet and Greet, then purposely planned for me to take the poisoned medication and oversleep, missing the opportunity to meet and marry Evan Gallagher. It had to be the latter, since that's exactly what happened.

I went ballistic.

Pacing madly through the house, breaking things along the way, I ranted and raved. When Miss Poopsie crossed my path I kicked her in the ass, which sent her airborne into the hall. Not seriously injured but fearing for her life, the cat ran to hide in the top of the open closet, secluding herself on the top shelf behind Greg's bowling ball.

Lemonade schnapps flowed over ice cubes, and still I ranted. "You stupid fuckin' bitch! You goddamn Scottish soap star hating whore!"

I'd been pacing like a sideshow cougar, but paused long enough to drain half the glass.

"First you pretend to be my friend. Then you ruin my life and make me miss my wedding day with Evan! You even made me kick my fucking Poopsie, who I love so goddamn dearly! Aaaaagh!"

The remote control smashed against the wall, shattering into shards of plastic that flew across the room.

"Tonight, your ass is mine!"

Chapter Twelve

The distance between insanity and genius
is measured only by success.
~Bruce Feirstein

I turned off the headlights and waited, parallel parked across the street from Corkers. Very soon, I expected Lori to emerge in front of the liquor store for a cigarette break. There was only an hour and a half before the Friday night closing time of 1 a.m.

I stroked the shillelagh lying across my lap, wishing I could've used it again tonight. I had a strict personal policy of never killing two people in exactly the same way, so bludgeoning Lori with it was out of the question. I opened the chamber of Greg's Smith and Wesson revolver, spun it around, checked to make sure all six of the newly painted green bullets were snuggled in their sockets, then snapped it shut. I picked up the duct tape and empty water bottle from the passenger seat, then taped the empty drink container to the end of the pistol barrel. A homemade silencer resulted, thanks to a Google search I'd made that afternoon. I put the gun down in the seat and turned on the radio.

Now for my alibi. I dialed Greg, cell phone to cell phone, and was glad to hear him pick up. "I'm on my way to town to pick up some kitty litter. You need anything from Walmart?"

He asked me to grab a frozen pizza, inadvertently helping in my clandestine plan. I jotted that down in my memo pad. The list would be valuable evidence, should it come to that.

I watched the front door of the liquor store waiting for Lori to come out. It couldn't be much longer. "Hate My Life" played on the radio and I sang along, trying to keep my voice to a whisper. I love that fuckin' song!

Eight minutes later, Lori emerged through the front door and lit up a Marlboro. She leaned against the building and took a long, deep drag.

The car window was already down. Night shadows hugged the Buick and obscured me from view. I was so glad I'd bought Greg the cool laser sight last Christmas, one of the best buys I'd ever made on eBay. I had very little experience with firearms but with this nifty gadget affixed to the revolver, all I had to do was aim the red dot and fire. Lori was oblivious to the crimson spot glowing between her eyes as she exhaled the last puff of smoke from her lungs.

I squeezed the trigger. A muffled pop sounded. The homemade silencer worked pretty well.

Lori slid to the ground, gore and brain matter marring the glass door behind her. I think she died instantly, without knowing a green bullet had pierced her brain. I should've aimed a little to the left, to make her linger long enough to feel remorse for what she'd done.

"Woo hoo!" I was elated. "Rest in peace, you racist bitch! Viva la Ireland!"

I cranked the car, but left the headlights off until I'd circled the block, at which point I drove the blue Buick toward the bridge back into Evansville.

I tossed the homemade silencer, tape still dangling from it, into the trash can on my way into Walmart. Humming a happy tune, I tossed kitty litter in the cart beside the frozen pepperoni pizza. A few of the late night patrons looked at me strangely as I laughed. I'd just noticed the bag contained Irish Spring scented kitty litter and featured an adorable little cartoon leprechaun dancing a jig with a cat on the front. The thing that nearly made me piss my pants was the shillelagh in his hand. Oh, I wish I could've used this brand in Harry's Hefty bag shroud!

The sales clerk chatted with me as she rang up the purchase, asking if I had a cat. It was late, the girl was getting sleepy, and idle chatter made the night pass more quickly.

"I have a cat named Miss Poopsie, but not one of them," I answered, pointing at the drawing of the leprechaun. "Leprechauns aren't real, you know."

"Okaaaay." The girl blared her eyes before she gave me change. I guess her contacts were dry or something. "You have a nice night."

"Thanks, and you have a great night too!" I folded the receipt before putting it in my purse for safekeeping. I might need it to prove I was shopping about the time Lori was shot.

No one had been around, there were no security cameras outside the liquor store, and my car had been hidden under a veil of darkness. Plus, I was used to getting away with shit like this. When the mailman went missing, the post office had phoned people on my street to ask if we'd received mail the day he disappeared. I'd said I hadn't. The police never questioned me. I read a short missing person paragraph about him in the back of the newspaper a few days later, but that was the end of it.

I went home and ate half of the pizza I bought for Greg while I watched the video for "Hate My Life" on the computer. I don't usually go for dudes with sleeve tattoos, but the lead singer for Theory of a Deadman is smokin' hot!

I went to bed and slept like a baby. Life is good.

Chapter Thirteen

There is a pleasure, sure, in being mad,
which none but madmen know!
~John Dryden

The next day I opened a can of tuna for Miss Poopsie, who was still walking a bit crooked after having her ass kicked across the room. Silly cat ought to know better than bother me when I'm in a bad mood, but I love her anyway.

My mind turned to the missed Nashville trip. I retrieved a box of stationary from a kitchen drawer and sat down to write Evan a letter of apology. With a red gel pen, I filled in all the space between the snake and butterfly emblazoned borders. Promising to try my best to meet him soon, I explained that my psychotic former friend was to blame for my missing the Meet and Greet. I signed it 'Forever yours, Your Bride-to-Be, Judith.' I dotted the 'i's with tiny hearts.

After a few minutes of hectic daydreaming, I added a postscript telling Evan I hoped he liked the gift I was sending, a small token of my undying affection. I ran to the bedroom and searched through my top dresser drawer. Unable to find what I sought, I remembered it was in the laundry. Minutes later, seated back at the kitchen table, I sealed up a small box that contained the letter, spritzed with some of my most seductive perfume, and the lacy red panties I'd fished out of the hamper. With a red marker, I printed the address for the *Heartbeats and Teardrops* fan club.

That was one time I actually missed Harry Qualls. He may have been an asshole, but at least he could be trusted to deliver the things I put in the mail, when he wasn't busy pissing all over my stuff. The new twit they hired to take his place was a total moron who delivered almost nothing but bills and junk mail addressed to somebody named 'Resident'.

I remembered how wonderful it'd been to see that stupid bitch, Lori, with her Scottish brains splattered all over the place. I felt such a rush, I put in one of my exercise videos and had fun burning off the energy that coursed through my veins.

I was still jazzed up that evening at work. My job didn't suck any less, but I was in a good mood. I even lowered myself to straighten up the candy shelves. A small container of antifreeze had spilled in the automotive isle, so I actually mopped up the mess and put the open jug in the trash can behind the counter. I was careful not to spill any on my new Theory of a Deadman T-shirt I'd bought at the mall that afternoon.

The store was slow so I grabbed a magazine from the Rock 'n Roll section and a bag of chips, added a big splash of peppermint schnapps to my plastic cup, and took a seat behind the register.

The door chimed as a man with a young daughter entered the Gas 'N Go. "This way, Jillybean." He grabbed some beer and steered his six-year-old away from the candy isle and toward the slushie machine.

"That sure was a shame about that girl from the liquor store," he said, placing a newspaper on the counter beside their drinks. "I hate to think something like that could happen here, right down the street from where I live."

Something about that last sentence made me nervous. No one could possibly have seen what I'd done, but a voice in my head said this man knew.

"Yeah, what a pity." Trying my best to look inconspicuous, I picked up a feather duster and started cleaning the overhead cigarette display. "I think I heard somebody say it was a gang of disgruntled Scotch people or something."

"I need two of those lottery tickets, too," he said, pointing to the little cards with the green dice on them.

"Sure thing. Have we met before?" I tried to find out whether this guy really did know something or was just fucking with me. "I was wondering if I look familiar to you . . . at all?" I handed over the lottery tickets and anxiously watched the customer whose response could greatly affect both our lives.

"I don't know, maybe. In a town like this, we're liable to run into each other once in a while, I guess."

My mind shifted to overdrive.

The little girl's tongue had turned blue from her slushie. Her dad's was half empty. I felt my eyes glitter in their sockets as I took a swig from my schnapps filled cup.

"Here, let me get you a drink holder for those. Wouldn't want you to spill 'em on the way to your car." While the man scratched off his losing tickets, I grabbed their cups and squatted down behind the counter, out of view. One hand grabbed a drink holder as the other reached for the trash can. I sloshed a generous amount of antifreeze into his drink before standing back up with the refreshments. I remembered seeing warnings about antifreeze poisoning at the vet's office. If the stuff was good enough to kill a St. Bernard, it should work just as well on this nosy tattletale.

I rang up the merchandise and sent them on their way.

When the door closed behind them, my worries were over. I wished I'd found out his name so I could've added him to my shit list.

Whistling "Hate My Life", I went back to my magazine, sipping my schnapps as I turned the glossy pages. When I got back home, the first thing I was going to do was look up the lead singer's name. I had a feeling he'd be thrilled shitless to meet me.

Epilogue

Judith lived out the rest of her life as free as a bird, never suspected of her worst transgressions. She died of liver problems fourteen years after Lori McClanahan's unsolved murder.

Greg Webster outlived his wife by three years, dying quietly in his sleep as he dreamed of riding down the highway with Judith, the love of his life.

After they died, their home changed hands a few times before being bought by Jim and Tabitha Bauer, a nice young couple with two small children and a Yorkshire

terrier named Snookie. One fall they decided to have the chimney cleaned to get rid of
the nests left by birds the previous summer. The kids loved to roast marshmallows
by the fireplace, and their mother was
afraid stale bird poop might fall down and
become an unsavory filling in one of their
s'mores.

The chimney sweep made an odd discovery when finishing up the job. Some of
the bricks had fallen out to reveal a cubby
hole hidden in the fireplace. Human curios-
ity urged him to feel around inside. He
withdrew a stack of memo pads held together with old rubber bands, a nubbin of a
pencil still tucked securely into one of the
spiral bindings. He blew off a layer of dust,
then handed them over to the lady of the
house along with his bill.

Tabitha Bauer flipped through the small
tablets not knowing what to make of them.
Each had the words 'Shit List' written on
their covers. Page after page held hundreds
of crossed out names, including a few famil-

iar ones.

Harry Qualls had been her mailman when she was a little girl; she remembered he used to bring her tiny chocolate bars around Easter and Valentine's Day. It was odd to find her great uncle's name on the list as well. Larry Fulkerson had died in a freak wood chipper accident the year before she was born. Her grandmother said a million times that she suspected someone pushed him in to the contraption, but the police had never given it a second thought.

She snapped the old rubber bands back around the weird notepads and tossed them into a drawer. If nothing else, they'd make a great conversation piece during the dinner parties she liked to throw.

Tabitha grabbed the bouquet of daisies she'd bought that morning and headed for the door. Best to get the cemetery trip over with before the kids got home from school.

Today would've been her little sister's birthday. She might have been dead herself, had she not been visiting her aunt on the night her father poisoned Jill's fountain drink with antifreeze. "May you rot in your jail cell, Daddy."

Judith's Favorite Schnappstails

Queen of Schnappstail
½ shot of apple schnapps (1.5 TBSP)
½ shot of peach schnapps (1.5 TBSP)
12 ounces of Sierra Mist or other lemon-lime soda
2 maraschino cherries

Pour Sierra Mist over ice and cherries, stir in the schnapps, and drink up.

Drunken Leprechaun
Guinness beer, one 12-oz serving
1 pony shot (2 TBSP) of caramel apple schnapps (Or use half apple and half butterscotch schnapps)

Add schnapps to a frosty mug of Guinness, give a quick stir, and enjoy.

1 shot = 1 jigger = 1.5 ounces = 3 Tablespoons
A pony shot = 1 ounce = 2 Tablespoons

Acknowledgements

I'd like to thank my friends at TheNext-BigWriter for being the first to read *Queen of Schnapps* and encouraging me with their critiques, advice, and feedback, especially the following: Nathan B. Childs, Patti Hauge, Jeanne Bannon, T Cat Taylor, Jim Bourey, and Lucy Crowe. And hats off to everyone in the Louisville Romance Writers, an inspiring group of talented writers from whom I've learned so much.

My appreciation goes to Nicki Kuzn, my copyeditor, for catching all those pesky typos and offering her expert advice.

Special thanks to my family and friends for putting up with me through all my endeavors. Heaven help you, since y'all are at least partially to blame for my twisted sense of humor.

My undying gratitude goes out to all my readers. Thank you so much for your continued support and encouragement.

About the Author

Photo courtesy of Brittany Hayes

Tina D.C. Hayes writes romantic suspense and cozy mysteries with a paranormal twist. She lives down a little country road in western Kentucky with her husband and four children. A few pampered pooches and two parrots keep her company while they stand guard against writer's block. In her spare time she reads, hangs out with friends and family, watches movies, plays guitar, and indulges her inner Foodie in the kitchen and by chowing down at cool restaurants. Currently up to her elbows in diapers, she's an expert at 4 a.m. bottle feedings and Patty Cake.

Contact Links

http://tinadchayes.wordpress.com
https://www.facebook.com/TinaDCHayesAuthor
https://twitter.com/Tina_DC_Hayes

Other Books by Tina D.C. Hayes

Rock Candy Romantic Suspense
Nefarious
Harlie's whirlwind romance with a rock star pisses off a jealous stalker hell-bent on having the object of his obsession all to himself.

Petal Pushers Mystery Series
Poison, Perennials, and a Poltergeist
Darci Shelton has just one year to make her new flower shop a success, but she must come to terms with the store's resident ghost while struggling to put Petal Pushers in the black.

Secrets, Snapdragons, and a Spirit
Darci tries to help a woman reclaim her rightful name and inheritance by uncovering dark family secrets someone may have killed for. Miss Addie is eager to help, but a

ghost can only do so much.

Grudges, Goldenrods, and Ghosts
An old cookie tin buried in the cellar under Petal Pushers leads Darci to a secret someone intends to keep hidden forever.

Novellas
No More Tears
Lisa must overcome her protective instincts after her sister is sentenced to death by cancer and focus on helping her enjoy the short time she has left.

Valentino, Be Mine
Sparks fly when two people who can't stand each other wind up looking after a rambunctious Yorkie who needs a new home.

Short Stories
"Midnight Reveille"
Lily doesn't understand what's going on when she wakes up to find an unexpected visitor in her room in the middle of the

night.